THE gEUCALYPTUS TREE

Vijayalatha N

Anecdote
Publishing House
For the love of quality reading!

Anecdote
Publishing House
For the love of quality reading!

Anecdote Publishing House
E-35-A, E Block, Gali No. 2 Ganesh Nagar,
Pandav Nagar Complex Delhi-110092

Published by Anecdote Publishing House

Published : January, 2022

ISBN : 978-81-95251-81-0
MRP : 299

Book Promoted and Marketed by Champ Readers Pvt. Ltd.
Illustrations by Aarohi Bhatt
Cover by Ragesh Puthiyedathu
Layout by Ashwani Kumar Sinha
Printed by Thomson Press (India) Ltd, New Delhi

Dedicated to all children, the plants & trees,
the great beings & the SUPREME Creator.

ACKNOWLEDGEMENT

This book isn't formulated within a day or a month, it's the by-product of ideas, thoughts and ideologies I accumulated over the course of time. This book is an attempt to share those amazing thoughts and ideas with the readers that might add value to their life. None of this would have been possible without the constant support of people Iam surrounded with.

I would like to thank everyone who has been part of this amazing journey. Extend my deepest gratitude to my family and especially my daughter Vrinda, for being my first critique and providing valuable inputs.

I would also like to thank my amazing friends for being there and owning me. This journey would not have been this smooth without your constant support. Special mention to the team 'Misty Mountain Home Stay' where I wrote most of my book.

Many thanks to Sagar & Ashwani from Anecdote publishing for being that sounding board and I thoroughly enjoyed working with them. Aarohi Bhatt is a fabulous illustrator and thanks to her for making this book come alive with her illustrations. Special thanks to Ragesh Puthiyedathu for giving life to the abstract concept in my head which is now the cover page of this book.

...and most importantly to my Master & the great beings who have guided me throughout and for many more to come.

CONTENT

CHAPTER - 1

IT'S ALL OUR MISTAKE

"It's all our mistake!

We did this to him", cried Neil's mother waiting outside the psychiatric ward.

"He will be fine Natasha! We will handle this together", consoled Neil's father with tears rolling down his eyes as he held her hand.

"How could we never see this coming Nirvan? I gave him a phone to see videos so I could get some time to complete my work. We got him the tab so he can learn but he got addicted to those damn games. He hasn't ingested anything nor slept in the last 48 hours! I did this to him! To ensure he eats well I ended up feeding the screen instead of food, remember we gave him phone or TV just to keep him engaged while we were busy taking a nap, also those weekend parties at home…ohh no ..oh nooo…. How irresponsible we have been as parents, absolutely ignorant and selfish" Sobbed Natasha uncontrollably as Nirvan stood there frozen, realising all the little things they ignored in their parenting.

This is a present time story of our contemporary days. A story of a whirling mind of a dear-ling who no longer is a happy-ling. This is the tale of Neil who squalled and bawled, yawled and howled over a ten inch screeny-weeny-gadgety which was now in a trash-ea-tin-ity.

DR·A·K

About three and a quarter years ago the nine-year-old Neil unconsciously got addicted to video games and internet. The unaware parents who casually introduced gadget to their quick witted and intuitive child for the purpose of education and entertainment had never anticipated such uncontrolled compulsive usage. They both were working parents and it took a while for them to realise what was befalling in his life. It all started with complaints of pain with extreme irritation in eyes. Upon doctor's evaluation they learnt that his eyes had become photosensitive. But this was only the beginning, the games he played were violent which resulted in nightmares and bed wetting. His world was a simulated three-dimensional virtual environment in which the day began with a new score while the night ended with a new high score upgrading to a brand new level in his video games.

After diagnosis by many doctors about Neil's addiction, his parents refrained him from using the screen which antagonised him deeply. Neil was weary of the constant lecturing on not using phone, not playing video games and not even spending more screen time. He revolted with a conviction that the whole world is integrated by this technology and banishing him from using it is pure evil. Excessive games not just led to the addiction but also to acute depression syndrome. Upon incessant request, they mutually agreed for a one-hour allowance of television or a game per day with no usage on weekends.

Last one year has been a tough journey for the entire family. Neil's parents made many changes to their own lifestyle to set an example for him. They used phones only for the purpose of work and kept it away as soon as they were done for the day. It was tough in the beginning but they worked hard to change their own subtly compulsive habits, to be present with him not just physically but emotionally and mentally too.

Their misery worsened when they started feeling guilty for what they did unknowingly. They put their heart and soul to make it work again, to ensure Neil lives a normal life just like other children, to be happy, playful and joyful. In a world where everyone can connect by click of a button this family was perhaps working very hard to establish a deeper connect with their own little child. No matter which era we live in - food for thought for all of us is - '*Are we truly connected?*'

CHAPTER - 2

CLICK THE RESET BUTTON

"I am recommending a course of antidepressants and a sedative that will help him sleep better", said Dr. A.K. with a deep sigh.

"We want him more alive, Dr. A.K. All these medicines are making him more tired. He is a smart boy, he created his own games and learnt programming at the age of seven. There has to be something better than this", questioned Neil's dad.

"Misuse of technology has torn apart many families, Nirvan. We have advanced but not learnt to balance. You both discovered your own subtle addictions which you never knew existed before. It's going to take time my friend. However, I have seen in my decades of experience that people can change when exposed to nature. It has its own magic, you see. You can try a change of place, more greener, new school, new friends, an entirely brand new environment for Neil. Just click the reset button! You never know… it might work", suggested Dr. A.K.

"But where do we go? We have everything here", interrupted Neil's mother.

"Life is a result of choices. Make one right choice and that changes everything for us! Ever heard of the butterfly effect? Give him something real!"

"We have done everything so far! We will try to consider this option too. Thank you Dr. A.K.!" said Nirvan in a soft tone as they dispersed from his office.

The strong-willed parents wanted to turn the table around. They were ready to adapt, to modify everything that could make Neil a happy child. Enroute their home, Nirvan and Natasha spoke at length about suggestions from Dr. A.K. on reset and change of place as Neil was fast asleep in the back seat.

"It's almost mid-term Nirvan, will we get admissions now?"

"I don't think even schooling matters at this stage. If he recovers well, I am willing to risk a year or so,. I am going to talk about remote working for a year at work so we can plan our relocation to a nice place".

"Would a year be good enough?"

"Let's start, will see where we get with it. Hey, where was that vacation where Neil was the happiest and without gadgets for an entire day?", asked Nirvan.

"That was the most memorable day in Ooty. It was an amazing resort, such a beautiful view.

Remember how Neil kept jumping from windows and we were chasing him".

"That was fun. That place was magical. Why don't we go there? We can afford the cost of living there and it's lush green." Suggested Nirvan.

"Ok...", said Natasha in a not so convincing tone.

"I know you are very worried and it's not easy for me either, but my heart says it's worth giving a shot, at least better than these drugs he is on. I will find out about school admissions too. Let's plan our relocation by the end of September", said Nirvan in an assuring tone.

"I'm just scared and worried. It hurts me to see him go through this pain. I just pray for some magic to happen", said Natasha with tears rolling down her eyes.

We all know of new beginnings, but we probably discount the past that triggered these new beginnings. Conventionally it takes a plethora of courage, perseverance, patience, and immense love to endure the process of change. Sacrifices of parents are so easily discarded, however their love is so immense that they can turn-the-tide for their children. However, at this stage Neil was not in a condition to appreciate nor acknowledge the sizeable swap his parents were making only for him as they shifted to an entirely new place.

CHAPTER - 3

THE SHADOW GIRL & THE COLOUR CUBE

The new neighbourhood was quiet and lush green, filled with radiant colourful flowers. The cool temperate weather was gratifying for Natasha and Nirvan which gave them hope during their taxing times. Their new house in Lovedale, Ooty was a three-bedroom bungalow with a dining hall, large living room, spacious kitchen and a sit-out area opening to the backyard with giant eucalyptus trees. It had a plenty of garden space with varieties of flower in a two-acre property. It had a stone wall fence shared with an almost invisible neighbour, who never even ventured to check-in since their arrival three weeks ago.

New place did not have the same influence on Neil as it had on his parents. He was mostly gloomy with absolutely no interest in doing anything which was also accompanied by tantrums for accessing screen to play games. The antidepressants which he was on, didn't help him either, he was mostly bitter than better. Neil used the smiley dictionary, gaming lingo, abbreviations and his own gibbrish expressions in his normal interactions which was something very unusual for the folks at his new school. His teachers in the new school had already started sharing feedback on his peculiar ways of speaking. The teachers believed that using it in everyday interaction would cease his natural expressions. They were also very concerned about Neil's antisocial behaviour tagged with constant depressive state which his parents defended as an effect of the new place and assured he would be better in days to come.

It was about 11 pm on a Wednesday night when Neil walked to his parents' room, grumbling on top of his voice,

"Why can't I have my own phone? Rest of my classmates have their own smartphones. It's so embarrassing! I can't play games or watch television anymore. Everyone is learning how to use them!"

His parents who were getting almost settled in bed for a good night sleep were shaken up by his tone, while Neil continued with his grumpy expression and high tone,

"I want my phone! All children play with their friends! I want my friend back! This INH.."

"INH?" inquired Nirvan,

"It means 'Its Not Happening'. Baby there is no friend on the phone", replied Natasha in a soft tone as she kneeled down to hold him by his shoulders.

"You are lying! My virtual assistant is my best friend. He is always there for me. I feel like nobody without him!" cried Neil.

"Oh Neil! Look at me. That app is not your friend. You have to make some real friends", explained Natasha in a gentle tone while Nirvan stood beside him.

"My heart is broken, you don't love me anymore. You always listen to that pyssss..cii..arrrt Dr. A.K.. I hate you!" sobbed Neil as he ran back to his room.

Neil was petrified and disconsolate. He was subjected to many does and don'ts. He was prohibited from using his phone and playing video games. He was allowed to watch television only for two hours a week. This protocol by his parents had left him completely distorted and disgruntled. Well, he was addicted! Despite all the counselling he underwent, he could not get off the screen.

"I will handle this. You go to bed", said Nirvan to Natasha as he walked to Neil's room.

As he entered his room, he spotted him gazing outside the window sniffling and wiping his tears off. Nirvan watched him in silence from the door as he was caught with some endearing sight which was helping him settle down faster. After about fifteen minutes later, Nirvan left without interrupting him.

Neil saw a child playing outside on the lawn in the neighbouring house. The dim street light did not help him get a clear view either. He wiped his glasses and gazed again. This child had two pigtails.

"*Fizz - O - Dizz*! Why is this girl playing out at this hour in the night?" he questioned himself.

It was pitch dark and all he could see was a girl-like shadow figure with two pigtails who jumped very high in the air. It almost appeared like she could fly. After several minutes she sat down to play with a colourful squarish cube-ish thing in her hand when she caught the attention of Neil peeping from his window. She glanced at Neil with curiosity and swiftly jumped over the fence very effortlessly to walk towards his window.

She had no face! No eyes! No nose or lips! She had hands and legs with a long neck but she was a three dimensional shadow. It was too quick for Neil to react. He stood frozen at the sight of this girl. She took the small colourful cube and placed it in the window pane. Numb Neil was dumb struck. He could not utter a word. Astounded, he

opened the window slowly and picked up the cube while the girl stood by the pane. He remarked in a soft tone, *"Shadow Girl!"*

The girl's face expanded the way people with faces would do when they smile. Neil bent closer to get a view of her expanding face and so did she. A voice spoke, "Are you sad?"

Neil freaked out at this voice, he instantly shut his window and pulled the curtain, then jumped into his bed covering himself completely. After a few minutes he plucked up the courage to peek out of his blanket to get a glimpse of *the shadow girl*. She was now standing inside the room watching him. He had innumerable questions running in his head, how did she come inside when the window was closed? Why is she out so late at night? Where is her face? Who is she?

"So many questions!! I come here to play when it's asleep!" replied *the shadow girl.*

"Err....you mean your mom"

"No, she is not my mom ...she is M......I got to go....it's awake"

"What, hey wait! What do you mean by It's awake! What are you referring to?"

He jumped from his bed to check what was awake. From the window he noticed the light in her house was switched on. *The shadow girl* was starting to fade away, he felt that a monster who lived in that house had captured this poor girl and took away her face. He gazed and dazed as he was crazed being so amazed until *the shadow girl* who was unfazed, bid him an adieu as she disappeared in the thin air. Bemused, he went to his bed pondering over the shadowy-ling, the colourful cube and the monster in that house.

CHAPTER - 4

THE SCIENCE PROJECT

Neil woke up to his mom's voice to get ready for school. He peeked out of his window harking back to an encounter with *the shadow girl.* A lady in her possible early forties walked out of the main door from *the shadow girl's* house talking over the phone. She sat outside on her patio with a cup of hot brew in her hand. Very disinterested, he got ready in his typical disconsolate ways with a gloomy face and walked to school with his father.

As a consequence of lack of sleep he hit the sack early, however his deep sleep was interrupted by a knock on his window. With heavy eyes he turned around to see two square shaped flashing lights. One was yellow while the other was bright green which changed the colours on his window screen. Curious, he walked towards the window and noticed that *the shadow girl* was flashing those lights with an almost invisible torch. He heard the same voice again, "Are you sad?"

Neil didn't say a word but stood still with his dejected looks watching her.

She walked closer to him keeping the chip size flashlight device on his window pane and flew away again. Every night for the next few days she knocked at Neil's window asking only one question, "Are you sad?"

Neil was so used to her coming and intruding his sleep every night that he would wake up at 11 pm on his own and wait for her to knock. But one night she did not turn up. He waited for a few hours and she never turned up. He felt sad, very sad. His gloomy face was gloomier than ever. He woke up on his own next morning, grabbed the cube in his hand and ran out through the back door to get a glimpse of *the Shadow girl.* He stood by the fence probing her lawn wondering where she was.

His rail of thoughts were interrupted by his mom as he heard her call out his name several times.

"There you are! You got me so worried. You are getting late for school, come get ready".

A little lost with the thought of *shadow girl*, he just followed his mom as she walked inside with a cube still in his hand.

"Neil, that's a 7X7 Rubik's cube. Where did you find it?" asked his mom in surprise.

"*The shadow girl* gave me".

"*Shadow girl*? Hmm, you should introduce us to her next time".

"How is your science project coming together Neil? Just two more weeks until the submission?

Did you decide what you will make?" enquired his dad.

"Solar system! But I don't feel like doing anything", said Neil in a low voice as he left for his school still lost in thoughts of *the shadow girl.*

After a stodgy monotonous day at school, his arrival at home was startled by the presence of *the shadow girl* in his room, sitting on his study table doing something. He was happy to see her in relatively odd timings than her usual midnight visit. *Shadow girl* turned around with an expanded face as if she was smiling and pointed towards a beautiful 3D model of the solar system. Each planet in a perfect sequence of colours. Saturn had wonderful rings and three additional planets than what school books say. She touched the sun, and the entire solar system model was set in motion just the way it was written in books about planets own rotation in their orbits.

"How did you do this?" asked wonderstruck Neil.

"Is Neil happy now?"

"How is this even possible? There are eight planets, right? What are these three planets that you added? *Fizz - O - Dizz*!!! You also got the dwarfs, asteroids and comets here?

Fizzz - O - Dizzzzzzz!!! This is a live Solar System? How did you even do that *Shadow girl?*

"Is Neil happy now?"

"I am just astonished! How did you do that in real life? This happens only in a virtual world", he said in an excited tone.

"Is Neil happy now?"

"Of course! I'm so happy and where were you yesterday night?"

"I was busy working", said *the shadow girl* as she walked towards the window and jumped out waving a bye.

"Working? Hey! But wait! You didn't tell me.......?"

Neil was unhappy about *Shadow girl* leaving him but was equally flabbergasted at what she created. He called his parents to show the model. He went on explaining how *the shadow girl* did all this. He was smiling! He was excited! He was happy! He was talking and he was just happy!! It was a beautiful surprise for Natasha & Nirvan to see Neil not just talking about others but also smiling and being happy from head to toes. Happiest moment for them in a long time!

"Where does *the shadow girl* live, Neil?" asked Natasha curiously.

"There", said Neil pointing towards the neighbouring house.

"How lovely! I am glad you made friends with our neighbour. Why don't you share a gift with her? She would be happy too", suggested Natasha.

"Gift!"

"Yes, gift. Why don't you make something for her, just the way she made this solar system for you!"

"But what can I make Mom", replied Neil with a smile.

"You can make a thank you card with some colourful drawing to begin with. Come let me help you".

Three of them sat down with real colour pencils and paper in a very long time to make the thank you card for *Shadow girl.* Of the nine years of Neil's life, over three years were an unconscious life of addiction to the world of the phone. He was so lost in the virtual world that he never paid attention to these little things that could also bring joy. This was the first time in over three years he agreed with his parents for something other than a gadget or video game. The astonished parents were secretly happy with this tiny change. After the thank you card was ready they showed him some board games, cricket bat, ball, badminton and also different cubes which were in their storeroom and explained how he could use all these to play with *the Shadow girl.* They were overjoyed at this sight and wanted to encourage him to never let this little spark of joy go away.

Neil was happier, there was sudden shift in his personality, he was more active and always looking forward to meet *the Shadow girl*, she undoubtedly seemed to be doing some magic! While the parents were very happy about this, they were also wondering about who she is. On enquiry they learnt that quite an unsocial lady lived there alone, she travelled most of the times and had no children at all. While they never dismissed existence of the girl whenever Neil spoke about her however, they were a little concerned for sure after learning the facts of their neighbour. They were consistently in touch with Dr. A.K. and given the description of the girl and her abilities to fly, he wondered about the existence of this girl. Was she real or yet another creation of Neil's highly imaginative

THANK
you

mind? Was it his coping mechanism? But what could not be ignored was the presence of a Rubik's cube, the chip sized flashlight and the three dimensional model that was out of question for Neil to create it so quickly right after coming back from school!

CHAPTER - 5

MONSTER NAIR AND THE CHATTERING MIND

Neil's science project was highly appreciated by everyone at school. It was shortlisted for the best project of the year. Unperturbed by all the fame at school, his only interest was to know how *Shadow girl* could do all this. He was exhilarated and wanted to share everything that happened at school with her. On the way back home, he stopped by the gate of her house, on the right side of the gate 'Dr. M. Nair' was inscribed in bold on a black stone at the centre.

He called out, "Hey *Shadow girl*! Shadowwww girrrllll"

Upon not receiving any response, he opened the gate to an amazingly colourful garden, there were a different variety of plants, the narrow path to the patio had young saplings which he treaded on and trampled unmindfully before he rang the doorbell. A lady came by the window peeking out. It was the same lady Neil saw from his window sipping hot brew on her patio the other day. She lowered her spectacles with her right index finger, looked deep into her eyes and in a rude tone asked, "Whatttttt do you wantttttt?"

"Errr, I..I…I..am friend of th..th..the… *shadow girl*", stammered Neil as the lady's eyes grew three times bigger than her glasses.

The three-dimensional model of the solar system fell down from his hand at this horrendous sight of the lady. As much as he was scared he was very sad to have broken the model which *the Shadow girl* made for him. Neil was so upset that he felt like spinning this evil lady into a spider web and hold her captivated right inside the cocoon. He bent down to pick up the broken parts when he noticed a giant spider walking towards him, he jumped aside swiftly to realise what he just thought was turning out into a reality. The giant spider started spinning her in the web.

He screamed, "NO…nooo don't!"

"Don'ttttttt, what?" questioned the lady.

"Don't spin……oh my God! You are right here, what was that".

"That was you trying to spin me up in your head", the lady responded in a very unemotional tone.

"Whaatt?"

"You brokeeeeeeeee your model ….does that make you sadddddddd?"

Neil, who was still unsure of what was happening, nodded his head in shock. The lady moved her hands and in a second everything was fixed just the way it was, as if it never broke.

"How did you do that?" said Neil in a state of shock.

He reached out to touch the 3D solar system at the centre to check its rotations. The solar system started expanding into giant planets, they were humming, each planet humming a different note reverberating at a different frequency. All these planets and sun could breathe, they had a humming language of their own! The solar system expanded into the infinite cosmos as he saw himself at the centre of it. Neil was a very imaginative and visual child but all turning out real was a frightful experience for him. He thought that she is the evil monstrous creature camouflaged in a human body suit.

"No! Am not an Evilllllll camouflaged in a human body suit. I am Dr. M. Nair, you puzzled, dazzled, confused little brainnnnnn!" said the lady in a pride tone with her head held high.

"Doctor Mrs. Nair!"

"No!! Doctor M. Nair".

"Ok! Mrs. Nair".

"M. Nair".

"Ms. Nair".

"Ahh whatever, I am not an illusionist nor a witch. Now stop thinking crazy. Your mind chatters a lot. Do you want to come in for a tour of my house, it's very rare I allow people to come inside", said M. Nair with a wickedy one sided smile.

At this point Neil thought to himself, "Maybe this is exactly how the little girl got eaten up by this Monster Nair and all that was left was her shadow. She wooed her right inside the house and unaware of the awful intent the girl fell for this trap."

"I don't eat childrennnnnnnnnnn you chattery jittery head", exclaimed M. Nair in a sharp tone.

"Errrrrrrrr.....you read my mind. I should stop thinking".

"You should indeed stop thinking such ghastly things. Your mind needs a cleannnnnnnnnnnnn up just like my laptop".

Neil could see the junk folder popping up in air and deleting the junk files from brain system.

"*Fizz - O - Dizz!* Whatever I am thinking is turning out to be real. Stop this Monster Nair! I am afraid I will eat you up forever".

"You can never eat me forever, I am not one but many. The more you eat me, the more I clone and you can never know which one is real and which one is a clone. He ha he ha he ha ha ha ha ha ha he huaaa hhaaaa ha ah!" laughed M. Nair out so loud.

Watching her laugh, the frightened Neil brightened with a smile. He was dismayed but could not resist giggling. His lips moved left, then a little right, a little up, a little down, round and round up until his mouth opened wide and bursted into laughter. They both sat on the patio and laughed so hard that tears streamed down their eyes. His mother Natasha who stepped out to check on Neil as he was late to home was astounded at this sight. She too laughed standing by the gate watching them laugh. Natasha was happy to see this change in Neil, but was equally jealous that she could never make him laugh like that.

"Hey chatterrryyyyyyyyy boy, is that your mom by the gate in a state of shock? Your laugh seems to be the tenth wonder of the world in this millennia?" said M. Nair as she stood up to greet

her.

“Yes Monster Nair”, said Neil in a polite manner as he stood up to pick up his school bag and the 3D model.

“It’s veryyyyy nice meetinggg you Natashaaaa. I am Dr. Nairrrrr”, greeted M. Nair with a sweet smile.

“Mom how does she know your name?”

“It’s an honour meeting you too. I read about your articles and the great work you do with plants. We didn’t know we had an amazing neighbour until Neil spoke about your daughter”. Said Natasha ignoring Neil’s question

“My daughterrrrrr!”

“My son refers to her as *the Shadow girl*”

“Oh, Neil’s friendddddd, the Shadowww Girllll! Yes, we seemmmmm to likeeeeee Neil verrrryyyy much. He has a funnnnyyyyy way of thinkinggggggg”.

“We are glad he could make new friends here.”

“Oh waitttt, I got a gifttttt for Neilllllllllll”, Dr. Nair walked towards him and tied a pentagon shaped watch on his left wrist which had tiny buttons at the converging points of this pentagon and whispered softly into his ears "This is a *TTD*! It will helpppppp you keep your mindddd cleannn!

"Whats *TTD*?"

"Thoughtttt Tracking Deviceee! It will track all your thoughts that you generate during the day and all feelings or visuals associated with it"

"Oh wow thought tracking device like the GPS! What else it can do?"

"Figureeeee it outttttt *chattery boyyyy*?"

"Dr. Nair, this was not needed", intervened Natasha.

"We love Neillll! Perhaps thissss is what he needs nowww"

Natasha smiled reluctantly and with gratitude they both left Dr. Nair's home. In a world so infinite, we are often so trapped in limitations of our mind failing to infer how our mind functions. Neil kept wondering why his mind always chattered, what if everything he thought turned out to be true. What was this thought tracking device going to do? What if Monster Nair had already hacked his head and hence all this was happening. He was not scared of her anymore but amused and curious. He made up his mind to investigate the truth behind her witchy wickedy skills.

CHAPTER - 6

THE GENIE

Neil's never-ending thirst of curiosity triggered a completely new chain of events in his life. He began talking to a few other children in the neighbourhood to investigate the mysterious Nair which perplexed even his parents. No one knew about her whereabouts, where she came from, when she came to or left her home, what she ate or for that matter even her clothes were never seen dried outside. Talk of the town was that she was unsocial with others and locked up in the house mostly.

His suspicion grew stronger when he overheard a conversation about a nine-year-old girl who went missing and never turned up again. He now had an unsubstantiate evidence against Monster Nair on how she ate that girl and left her to be the residual shadow. He got his perfect moment when he noticed *Shadow girl* had not turned up for a week. It was a sunless sunday morning, he probed her house over the fence wall, the main gate was open however the newspapers along with milk packets were piled up near her main door.

He trampled on tiny saplings yet again as he hopped into the patio pushing the multiple pots planter stand which were full of blossoming flowers. He raised his toes and hands up to ring the bell to verify her presence at home but a walloping sound of smashed flowerpots and the planter stand jolted Neil. He didn't intend it to turn out like this and as worse as it can get he noticed agitated M. Nair gazing through her window through her glasses on the tip of her nose, witnessing the vandalization of her beautiful flower planterettes. Infuriated by the event, she opened the door angrily, marched sprightly and grabbed Neil by his ear.

"Aaahhh! Let me go", screeched Neil.

"I won't sparrrrreeeeeeeere you today Neil! You are such an awful, unhappy and grumpy child I have ever seen in my life!"

"Sorry M Nair, I am extremely sorry! I won't do it again".

"You don't meannnnnnnnnnnnn it! I need to bring your parents' attentionnnnnn to this".

"No, no, no, no! I will fix those flowerpots".

M. Nair dragged him inside her home. Unclasping his hands, she made him sit in the lounge chair placed in her beautifully assembled living room which had mysterious paintings with symbols and colours. Gazing deeply into his eyes with her hands crossed, she remarked, "It's the thirdddd time you have hurttttt my planttttsss since your arrivalllll. I am notttttt going to be kind this timmmmeeeee with you. Now, you sitttt here untillll your parentttts come to yourrrrrr rescue".

"I am very sorry, I will fix all these plants for you".

"Sounds like a deallll! But whattttt are youuu doing herrrrreeeee? Investigating eh.....whatttt I do, whennnn I come hommmme blah blah blahhhhh...."

"Errr I was just curious.... how.... did you do all that.... you know the spider.... the solar system... how did you do that.... The thought tracking device... it says my thoughts are living things... how is all this even possible?".

"Curiiiiiooooossssiiiiiitttyyyyyyyyyy............", stretched M. Nair in a very scary tone.

By now it was evident that mysterious Nair had a funnily horrifying way of speaking with a long stress on certain words which Neil seemed to be getting used to now. As she started speaking about curiosity, Neil was distracted by the big canvas paintings on the wall. He got so pulled into it that Dr. Nair's voice faded away as he walked closer to the paintings to get a better view.

The first one to get his attention was the black art with three dimensional whirls with a question mark at the centre and two parallel white lines both vertical and horizontal. It resembled a lamp from left, humans looking at each other from centre and as he walked to get the view from the right, he noticed a line of lights connected to a bigger painting which was filled with ancient symbols in circular manner around three triangles interlocked with each other which gave the appearance of a star, which in turn was connected to another bigger painting filled with lights made of magnificent colours which started shooting out lines of lights circling all over the room.

He touched the lights with his hand, it was warm and vibrating and it appeared as if they were alive talking to each other. The lights whirled into a medium sized bonsai pot which had seven small sized straight eucalyptus trees. He opened his mouth in complete surprise as he followed the lights to the roof where there was a magnificent giant circular light ball with a comparatively smaller light ball which spread across the entire roof. His muse was interrupted by Dr. Nair as he put her hands on his shoulder with uneven nails of her fingers as if she chewed on them for her meals, "I see you seeeeeeemmmm to like my paintingggggggsss!"

Neil looked at her in awe, "You made these? Who are you, Mysterious Nair?"

"I am a Genieeeeeeeeee who is both stuck inside and free outside the lamppppp at same point in time but I don't know which one of it is meeeee .... even me... I don't know.... if I am me or I am not me... from inside the looppppp I am everything but outside of it I am justtttttttttttt...."

"Hmmmmm...... that's kind of gibberish..... I don't think... I understand".

"It's like how you are stuckkkk in your world of gameeesss, without realising what's realll and what's unrealllll. You think your parents don't lovvvveeee you anymore, while your parentttts changed everything about them to give you everything because they lovvvvveeee you more than anythingggg."

"How do you even know this, is it this thought tracking watch? Are you tracking my thoughts!!"

"No chattery boyyyyyy!" and she touched the green dot on his watch which opened a virtual screen where all thoughts of Neil were stored. There were over thirty thousand violent thoughts, forty thousand sad thoughts and just about 4000 neutral thoughts but there were no happy thoughts. The tracker showed how he was polluting the world of thoughts thus attracting more sad and violent thoughts which effected more than a million people in a day. His vivid imagination was not constructive, it alarmed him immensely!

"Is this for real, I have such destructive thoughts, I have no happy thoughts?"

"Yessss!"

"How do I change this, Monster Nair?"

"Its simple mathematicssss! You have to minus bad and unhappppyyy thoughts plus or multiply happpyyy thoughts!"

"What about the piles of bad thoughts that are here how do I change it?"

"Delete those in your hearttttt."

"Heart?"

Their conversation was interspersed by hurried footsteps towards the patio.

"Mrs. Nair, please accept my sincere apologies for Neil's blunder. I learnt from his friends about the mangle it caused. We will replace the planterettes in the next two days", uttered

Natasha as she stood by the door.

"Oh that won't be necessarrrryyyyy! Neil has been very kindddd to offer me help to fix them. He promised to visitttttt me from friday this week when his Christmas holidays beginnnnn. See you at 7am then. What a joy for me to have the company of such a lovely boyyyyyyyyyyyyyy!"

Neil thought to himself, "As if I will be here on Thursday hah".

"Nah Nah Nahhhhhh, don't even thinkkkkkk of it Neil..... I will let all your secrets out..... starting from how you stole phone from an innocent girl in school, how you lied..... la la la", said M. Nair only in his head.

"Now she speaks in my head", he jumped right next to his mom with a straight face glancing at her sideways.

"I will see you on friday at 7 am", said Dr. Nair out aloud as she bid adieu to both of them.

Neil was both astonished and surprised while Natasha was happy to know that he not only offered to help fix her plants but also accepted his mistake. Neil was more than sure now that Monster Nair was mysteriously evilsh than one could imagine. He was equally scared and curious, but he had to find out what happened to *the shadow girl,* who was Monster Nair and fixing the plants gave him an opportunity to dive into the secret life of hers.

CHAPTER - 7

CACOPHONIES OF THE GREEN

As the golden rays of the sun permeated through the branches of the trees, Neil reluctantly dragged himself out from his bed to prepare himself for the untold mysteries of the first day of his Christmas holidays with the Mysterious Monster Nair.

"She is evil! She played through it, knowing all my secrets. Ah! She is blackmailing me, she placed this undetachable thought tracker on my wrist, she says interesting things but she isn't really the one who she pretends to be! She is a child eater! I will teach her a lesson for sure. What if she is a villainy mutant mind reader who installed the tracker in my head when she grabbed me by my collar? No wonder I was distorted until she made me sit on the chair in her luxuriously mysterious living room. The 'fresh water' she offered me must have been multifariously ingrained by nanoscopic bots. What if those strange plants in her garden are camouflaging mutants awaiting the signal to attack the innocent humans? I will destroy them with my Taser shockwave gun. Boom! I think mom is right. I should learn real Jiu-jitsu to bring down evil dwellers among us. Huyaaa haiiiiii!"

"Neil, who are you talking to! Are you ready?" called his dad while waiting outside.

"Yes, dad!"

Neil walked in with a determination of tearing down Monster Nair's detrimental plans of mass destruction. He sneaked inside her gate in a stealth mode with his Taser shockwave gun. This time more cautiously to not trample the secret buttons which were hidden at the base of these plants.

"Ahem! Ahem! You are thirty minutes lateeeee my dear. By the way, I can see you in your stealth mode with your Taser shockwave gun."

Dismayed with the vindication of his analysis about her, Monster Nair said, "Well yes, I did implanttttt those nanoscopic bots inside you with that fresh glass of waterrrrrr."

"Holy cow! I knew it. You are the evil mastermind!"

"Yes! Now get yourself to work, Neily Neil-e Neieeelll and re-pot these mutantttttt plants in the planterettes, back to where they belongggggg. I will be back in an hour to assess your performance. Darrrreeeee you mutilate them! Fun Flora-e-days", said Dr. Nair in a smirky tone as she walked into her house.

"I was right about her! She is very wicked. Wait

until I teach her a lesson. Huh! Where do I start from?" said Neil to himself.

The pink carnations caught his attention. His awestruck eyes were filled with a disposition of endearment. He steadfastly examined the twenty planterettes he had vandalised. Each had flowering plants in them. Neil began to identify each of them. It was almost like a personal connection.

"Red rose, Pink rose, Whitish-Pink rose, Daisies, Purple Bougainvillea. Oh my God! I never knew a Purple Bougainvillea existed on this earth. Whoaa! Look at you Aster. Wow! You are beautiful! Oh my! This is a pinkish yellowish greenish. Aahhh! This is certainly the mutant!"

He threw that plant up in the air and targeted his Taser shockwave gun to terminate it forever. His fingers were held lightly on the trigger waiting to pull as the mutant came into the target zone. But, as the power was at play the mutant pulled out a *wuper woaker wadrozinator* and saturated Neil in the di-hydro-oxidized nanoscopic particles. In no time he was floating in the *wadrozinator* web of the plant conglomerate. He closed his eyes tight for it to pass by. He discerned it was all real unlike his games.

"I am caught in the web of wobbling *wadrozinator*! They are weaponized with *di-hydro missiles*. This is happening for real! This is not my imagination! Help! Help! Monster Nair help!" he squealed in despair to find no help coming his way. His wailing was interrupted by a weird low pitch sound.

"gHa gHa gHa gHa gHa gHa gHa gHa gHa".

He opened his eyes facing up into the sky as he was being carried by these *wadrozinators* in the floating di-hydroxy web.

"Wait! Wait! Stop this! I truce with you. Can you see my imaginary white flag?"

"gNo"

"You mean no?"

"gYes"

"Truce! Please truce! I won't use my Taser shockwave."

"gYour gTaser gIs gNot gReal"

"Put me down please. I won't hurt you."

Neil shrunk himself to embrace the fall. He was just six inches above the surface and he didn't feel a pinch. Brushing himself off the grass and mud, he caught sight of the *wadrozinators*.

"Ahh! You are the flowering plants!"

Before he could say another word, Dr. Nair returned.

"So, you have been playing around and messing up my garden. You wasted all this water and scattered my plants!"

"No, M. Nair. It's them! These *wadrozinators* did it."

"Not one more word Neil! I want you back here tomorrow morning again at 7am unless you are ready to face the consequences!"

The cacophony of the *greenlings* who said everything with a 'g' rhymed with mockery and grockery. They laughed at him over and over again! He ran towards his house, ten feet away from Nair's, locking the gate, he sprinted to his room like never before. Every time he met her there was something new he was introduced to and every time he came up with extraordinary determination to face it with courage. The plants around and far off *gCacophonied* him until he drifted off to peaceful sleep.

CHAPTER - 8

THE gEUCALYPTUS TREE

It was just before the sunrise that Neil woke up to the cacophony of the *greenlings* again. He ran to his parents' room.

"Mom! Dad! Wake up! Can you hear these sounds?"

"What sounds? We can't hear any. Go to your bed Neil. These are your Christmas holidays and you are allowed to sleep a little longer", said Neil's mom.

"Hmm....No, I got to go to Mrs. Nair's. Have a good day!"

For all the obvious reasons, this certainly amused Neil's parents. But they were happy that Neil was doing something different.

Neil dressed himself carefully and walked into the core of the assorted *greenlings* from where the cacophony started.

"Look at you! You are an hour earlier today! And with your raincoatttt, umbrella. Woohooo! A real water gun! That's quite an improvementttttt!" mocked Dr. Nair.

"These are the safety measures from the *wadrozinators*. So, where do I begin today?"

"Here is the mud, manure and procedure to

re-potttttttt them. I hope you will complete it today. And hey! No matter what you do, don't go near the eucalyptus tree in the backyardddddddddd." remarked M. Nair as she gave the handout on procedure to Neil.

"Eucalyptus tree? I have never seen one!"

"Oh dearrrr! For that you need to step out of your screennnn. Such a pity! You know nothing about the plantttts around you. Well, for that matterrrr even humans in your neighbourhood. Have you ever had a petttt?"

"Oh yes! I had a pet dog in one of my games. I took very good care of her." Smirked Neil with great pride.

"Bligh me! You are ignoranttttt. Anyways, remember not to go nearrrr the eucalyptus treeeee."

"Yes, sure!"

While he agreed, his curiosity made him wonder why not? He sneaked into the backyard at snail's pace after the departure of Dr. Nair. The eucalyptus tree was right there in the centre of the backyard. It was remarkably herculean in its structure with a rare violet glow scintillating through every inch of its robust branches, circular leaves and gum infused bark. At the centre of the trunk was a seven spiral layer as if it was a gateway to its heart. Neil took a few pebbles from the fountain and aimed at the eucalyptus tree.

"gI gWouldn't gThat", uttered the young guava sapling.

"Hey *wadrozinators*! I got my gun today. Don't you dare to take me for granted! I will mutilate you all!"

"gFirstly, gYou gAre gAn gUnkind gChild gAnd gSecondly, gHe gIs gNot gWhat gHe gLooks gLike."

"What do you mean he is not what he looks like?" mocked Neil as began to throw the pebbles at the eucalyptus tree.

"gOh gDear! gYou gShould gNot gHave gDone gThat!"

The cacophony of the *greenlings* was interrupted by chimes of wind and a deep silence. Neil had never experienced such a silence where he could listen to his own breath and heartbeat. He saw a giant branch extending to him with all his pebbles, it had green leafy arms. He was terrified at this sight and started taking tiny steps backwards to escape. As he turned around to run, he was caught by the other branch which came right through Dr. Nair's main door. Neil screamed on the top of his voice.

"Ahhhhhhhhhhhh! Let me gooooo!"

He closed his eyes tightly as he was being dragged by the massive branch. He curled himself up as he felt that it was probably the last day of his life.

He murmured, "God save me! I am sorry for everything. I will never look at my phone again. I will play outside. I will listen to my mom and dad, never steal, never be sad, never harm anyone, I will minus all bad thoughts and plus good thoughts, pleaseeee save me!!"

The branches stopped moving after a few seconds. Neil relaxed his eyelids as peeped through the gap between his fingers that covered his face. His eyes hovered around to realise he was inside a giant tree trunk which bears resemblance to a home. It had a huge circular screen like object with a comparatively tiny gadget hung right next to it. It had seven colourful buttons and one tennis ball-size golden object at the centre. It almost appeared four times the size of a regular lotus flower. He recoiled his body and noticed that he was on a giant mattress made of dry leaves, seeds, twigs and some non-sticky golden green jelly-like substance underneath it.

His astonishment at the strange environment

multiplied when he spotted a probably eleven feet long bluish-green creature with human-like feet. He had long hands with eleven fingers each, a bright bluish-violet jelly wrap on his waist which covered until his knee, and a belly with five root like hanging woody spikes. Yikes! Human-like chest with tiny pores which were broader than normal humans, and a pair of eyes that resembled jelly beans with light golden and whitish-green sclera. He had a vertical and elongated violet pupil and his iris had a 360 degree vision. His nose looked like a circlish-squarish-triangle with a golden halo on his head and a big innocent smile on his face.

Neil jumped off the squeezy jelly mattress and clinged to the wall. He stammered and asked, "Who wh... whhhhooooo are you? I.. I… I need to go home! My mom is waiting for me……".

The bluish-green creature looked at the watch on his right wrist. He walked closer to Neil, bent down on his knees and held him by his shoulder. He looked into his eyes speaking in a hoarse low pitch voice.

"It's just 6:45 am of 24th of December. Your parents know you are here. All safe and fine!"

The touch of this weird creature felt smooth, soft

and nice to Neil. It was so calm that the fear was fading away. Neil pointed his index finger and touched his circlish-squarish-trianglish type of nose.

"Not quite scarier than you anticipated, eh?"

Neil bit his finger and murmured, "Are you for real? Who are you?"

"I am a being from the higher galactic realm! Several light years away from yours".

"Galactic? You are an alien? Oh my God! You must have the diabolic weapons that will destroy us all?"

"I am as alien to you as you are to me! In our realm, there is no weapon. We operate with our creator in very higher frequencies than on your planet collectively. Frequencies such as... hmmmm... guess the word in your planet is love".

Listening to this statement from the bluish-green creature, Neil comprehended that he would not cause any harm to him. His touch had the warmth that he felt when his mom cuddled him. He felt really relaxed, there was no chatter for the very first time in his head. He looked at his thought tracking watch, there were zero thoughts in creation at that point in time. He sat with his legs folded on a bunch of leaves, tapping his fingers on his cheeks. He looked into the eyes of the weird creature with amusement and wondered how it landed here.

CHAPTER - 9

THE CREATOR, CREATION AND THE ODYSSEY OF TIME & SPACE

"My name is Neil.
What is yours?"

"I don't have a name! In our realm, we are known by our uniqueness. But the little girl here calls me *Viridian*".

"*Viridian*! Because of your bluish-green colour?" giggled Neil.

"I suppose so".

"How and when did you land here?"

"Almost nine days and a few seconds ago of my galactic days. I was on an intergalactic trip for a key task but little did I know that my creator was in the process of building new galactic systems in the path of my voyage. The energy explosions of such systems are gigantic with enormous gravitational pull which hauled my *cosmogragnator* into one such burgeoning system. I had no control".

"Wait! You said the new galactic system. Is that a black hole? Did you say systems? There was more than one black hole? And what is cos..mo.. grag..naatrrr?" interrupted Neil.

"*Cosmogragnator* is something like your spacecraft. We are light beings and we use different bodies for various purposes, for our intergalactic travel we use *cosmogragnator*, just the way you use your body suits to execute your work on this planet"

"Bodysuits? No, this is who I am and all people …look, touch me and see".

"You all have lapsed your memory of who you truly are", remarked Viridan with a smile stroking Neil's hair.

"Wait, what do you mean? I am not what I look?"

"No, you are that which is inside this?"

"Huh! Impossible, anyways.... so the new systems you mentioned.... they all are black holes?"

"Ah yes, the new systems I cited are known as black holes to you beings on this planet. We call them the womb of the cosmos where life is growing. In the brobdingnagian cosmos, the creators of respective galaxies are constantly in the process of evolution, working along with the *SUPREME* creator to build the construct that accommodates expansion for future evolution of the cosmos itself".

"Your creator seems intellectually creative! My mom seems to be below average in comparison!"

"Haha! Little fella! My creator is both my mom and dad. Our creator is the same for all of us just like your God".

"We have many Gods here. But, I seem to like yours. It's pretty simple. So, what happened after you drifted into the black hole? Were you scared?"

"Our bodies are ascendant. They are programmed for resolution, safety, quick fix and result. We work with the galactic laws. Element of fear does not apply to us."

"Wow! Can I be like that? I am literally scared of so many things like my maths teacher, my exams, that fat bully guy at school, and I don't even go to the toilet alone at night."

"Maths teacher! Why would you be scared of her?"

"I hate her! She is very discouraging, always biased and supportive of that bully Ria in the class. I love maths but she complicates it. Children hate her except for Ria. Errrr…Sorry! I have been interrupting you. So, what was it like inside the black hole?"

"Inside that was high frequency incantations. It was expanding with colours of exorbitant vibrations. It was breathing faster as compared to my galaxy. The engine switched off on its own. I had no control over anything. After a while, the pull was very dense and I crashed at the foothills of a dense forest amidst the murkiness of the dawn".

"Whoops a daisy! Did you just say that the black hole was breathing, your galaxy breathed? You mean it was alive?" remarked Neil in an unbelievable tone.

"Everything in the *SUPREME* creator's construct is living, young being!"

"Hmmm……Were you hurt? How did you land in this tree?"

"I created this tree to lodge in until I fix my mutilated body and this *cosmogragnator.* Nonetheless, that was the start of mystic odyssey!"

"Odyssey! Wow! I want to listen to all of it!"

"gMe gToo", replied the guava sapling.

"gMe gToo, gMe gToo, gMe gToo", caterwauled the *greenlings* who peeped through the roots of the gEucalytpus tree.

"Yes, sure! But instead of narrating, I would rather show you what happened so that my little friend Neil gets clear visuals".

Viridian activated the giant circular screen by moving his fingers. Phosphorescent light hovered

around it, spinning in an anticlockwise direction and kaboom! It was the year of 1987.

"Wowww! This is like a giant television! Wait! How can you speak English? Do you speak the same language in your galaxy?"

"We don't speak words. Our communication is directly perceived by each other. Our bodies are inbuilt with extra sensory perception with an ability to acquire information about anything we come across. Therefore, I can converse in any language across any realm."

"Can you enable my ability to converse telepathically with you? Can you read my next question?"

"Inquisitive child! That ability is in each one of the creations. Some are masked while some unwrap their eternal attitude. I landed here nine days and a few seconds ago. This is the year 2022 for you but the time difference occurs as my galactic days are dissimilar in time than your Earth days".

Viridian took out a tiny fish pellet-sized grain and placed it right at the tip of Neil's medulla oblongata with a remark, "Just remember, what you will now experience will be a higher dimensional phenomena. You will feel, see, know, and correspondingly experience everything, all the events of my galactic days involving the details of all realms enroute. Since your body is incapable of this, I am inserting this *cosmogenic bubble* into your system to elevate you to greater dimensional reality. Please note there will be interference by limited emotions in your body until they get calibrated to this realm".

The giant television now spun clockwise from its centre whirling into the expanse. As the *cosmogenic bubble* inserted itself deeper, in a few seconds, Neil saw himself right inside the television waving back at himself while he was sitting inside the eucalyptus tree.

"gNeil gInside gTelevision! gWhich gOne gIs gReal?", remarked the greenling in awe.

"Look! The one out there on television is *gNeil* and I'am Neil, right here inside this tree! This is just like a cloning game", replied Neil in excitement

"gAwwwwwwwww!"

Neil and *gNeil* felt a complete pandemonium of voidness which annexed the pressure with fathomless darkness. He swirled and twirled while he curled and hurled, becoming this chaos itself. After several minutes his eyes opened to silence which spoke not in words but in light of colours which were supremely alluring in texture.

"How strange!" he wondered.

These magnificent colours were alive and existed not just around him but also within him. He looked around, he could feel the breath in everything even in hills, stones, and many others that were considered non-living on earth.

There was no gravity that applied any more. He strolled, trolled, and rolled until his gaze went skyward. Amidst the sky filled with multitude of vibrant lights, he spotted giant orbs surmounted by auric shield intersecting with each other as if they were singing, dancing and celebrating in continuum. Neil hovered upwards feeling the warmth of subtle currents coming by the way of the interjectory etheric shields.

"Oh My God! These orbs are the planets! They are alive! They breathe! They speak! Can you hear that? This is like my 3D solar system model which *the Shadow girl* made for me" said Neil from the tree in amusement.

Nodding his head he moved up further. There were layers of planets encircled at each level moving in conjunction at their own pace. There were diverse clusters which were similar to what we know as galaxies. Each sung and danced to the same song but with variation in their tone. Though they appeared separate from each other, oddly, they were synchronised. Right from above, all these formed the shape of a seven petalled flower with a core at their centre. All this originated from a core. The element of time was relative to all from the core but to the core it was all one.

"*Viridian*! The books say that the cosmos is chaos. But look, this is the most organized system. Time is non-existent and only a point of reference just like our metric systems. It holds no relevance in this continuum. The satellites or moons are evolving with their planets, breathing and alive, recreating and restoring itself. Why do I feel pulled to the core? Like it has known me ever since. Who is it?" enquired awestruck Neil.

"We refer to that being as *SUPREME* ! No one knows the name unless the *SUPREME* chooses to reveal himself".

CHAPTER - 10

THE LAPSE OF CREATION

Curiosity of the '*SUPREME*' was taken over by a strange phenomenal activity in its proximity at the perianth of Sixth and Seventh petal.

"Look! Something is happening at the base of the core!" exclaimed Neil.

"That's my creator from the sixth plane! What is he doing with the *SUPREME*? There is something they must be building or affixing that explains the lapse and my accident", expressed Viridan as he watched it with concern.

"Lapse! By the creator?"

"No Neil, they affix the lapse created by all of us from different realms collectively. Limited thoughts can cause quite a ruffle in the entire creation without us realizing it and the creators with their expertise are continuously making the amends to maintain the balance".

"We cause such massive imbalance? But how? Oh wait! Let me check my thought tracker?

He saw there were no bad thoughts created where *gNeil* was. He was so engrossed in the creation that there were only questions on creations, the colour of his thoughts were different now. They were brighter and connecting

with the cosmic colours. When he was in awe and happiness the colours were even more brighter and expansive. His amusement was paused when he saw the *cosmogragnator* arriving, "Look ..... *Viridian* you are on travel in your *cosmogragnator*. Can you change this?"

"I would not want to change this. There must be a reason for this, something I need to learn and accomplish here".

"How could you not be angry with your creator for putting you into this?"

"Since, I would have caused this for myself, it's my responsibility. I believe in working as a team with the creator".

"Oh no! *Viridian*, look, you are headed closer to the black hole!" said Neil with his eyes wide open.

gNeil caught sight of the *cosmogragnator* and *Viridian*. They both were swallowed in the lapse in a jiffy. The dimensional reality of the lapse did not have any impact on *gNeil* as he was non-partisan to this event. He swapped the planes of dimensional existence to realise he was back on earth. He set his eyes on the colossal eucalyptus trees encircling seamlessly far amidst the hills. The sun rays had just begun to filter through the earth's atmosphere but struggled to cut through dense cloudy mist of the Queen of hills. Strange as it could be, *gNeil* did not feel cold but Neil started shivering. *Viridian* wrapped his greenish-violet jelly blanket around Neil and with a snap of his finger, he materialised a chocolatey jelly cup with sparkles of silvery golden-white bubbles churning inside the cup. He cautiously offered it to Neil with a deep smile. The jelly cup was warm and it tasted as cosmic as *Viridian*. A crackling sound of branches followed by a loud thud interrupted his pace of scrutinization of the magical jelly cup of sparkling bubbles.

gNeil ran in the direction of the sound. He saw a gigantic *cosmogragnator* lying there at the crash site. Unlike the alien movies, this spaceship had not caught fire nor did it appear to be damaged. All that was visible was a bluish-metallic circular ship with black soot in some parts. Inspecting the ship to find the doorway, he spotted the same tiny remote-like gadget that was inside the eucalyptus tree with seven colour buttons and a tennis ball sized golden object at the centre resembling the cosmic realm of seven petals with *SUPREME* at the core. With his left forefinger, he touched the orange button followed by green, blue, violet, red, and yellow. And then kabooommmm! The *cosmogragnator* started

reverberating at lower frequency, augmenting into supersonic boom.

Neil screamed, "Hey! Move back from there! It's going to explode! My body can't handle it yet! Fly away right now!"

"You can perhaps control *gNeil*! He is you! Do not fear! Just focus, become him! Just like your games my dear!" said *Viridian* in a soothing and confident tone.

"Just like my video games?"

"Yes! But you will do that with your mind, not with remote. Hurry up!"

"*Viridian*! I.. I.. I… can't! I don't know!"

"What do you want *gNeil* to do?"

"Fly away from that radius!"

"Then just fly away in your mind! Time lag still exists by a few minutes between you and *gNeil*. This is your opportunity to zero the lag. Take control right now before you are hurt!" said *Viridian* in a strong tone.

With all might, Neil brought in his visualization and soon *gNeil* was gone from the explosion site to several miles away into the atmosphere with a sigh.

"OMG! I did it! I did that it!… did you see that *Viridian*…" jumped Neil in joy.

"gAwwwwwwwww!" exclaimed the *greenlings* while Viridan smiled holding him by his shoulders to give him warmth.

CHAPTER - 11

PATH UNKNOWN

The sonic boom had left Neil perplexed. However, he was now in extreme joy to experience real time gaming with increasing abilities of his mind.

The *cosmogragnator* started disintegrating itself into multiple eucalyptus trees as roosting birds rushed and gushed out of these. There was a complete silence radiating within the act of destruction as it started reintegrating itself into one herculean green trunk with scintillating violetish leaves. *gNeil* sneaked through the tiny spiral that formed at the centre of the trunk. An enormous blue body was taking the shape of the bark of the tree. The reverberation that was still quite intense produced massive electrical impulses generating several blue sparkling lines going out in the sky.

"gHe gIs gTrying gTo gCommunicate gWith gHis gCreator?" remarked the *greenlings* in awe.

gNeil hovered up quickly witnessing this amazing sight. Rude awakening as it could be, the blue sparkling lines were blocked from reaching the creator. As he inspected, he learnt that now even he could not crossover to that realm. All channels of communication were disrupted.

"Hey! Looks like you guys are having some

maintenance activity going on up there. There is a kind of explosion at the end of the seventh petal! Your messages never reached your creator as the portals were blocked. I can't go ahead either. Do you have any other way to reach out?"

Darkness spelled over *Viridian's* eyes. He appeared to be sad. With a sigh he said, "There is one way but no one has taken that path before. It's the shortest of all leading through the singularity of the spectrum to the *SUPREME*".

"Why don't you take that path *Viridian*? You could reach home sooner".

"The path to *SUPREME* is unknown. It is said that only the brightest of the heart can reach him quickly. I may have just two more days of my life left. Also, my heart isn't so bright anymore".

"Why isn't your heart bright anymore?"

"In my realm, the bodies live on the light of the creator of the sixth petal. It is the source of our food. But now, my body is taking its light from your planetary creator. Unfortunately, your planet is very young and already contaminated by very low emotions which don't vibrate at my levels. It's like a virus attacking my system. Unless my creator shares his light, my brightness will continue to fade!"

"How can you possibly die?"

"I don't die but my form sheds and my purpose remains incomplete! It will take a few years for me now given the contamination I am exposed to", said *Viridian* in a low tone.

"This is like stories of reincarnations on our planet!" said Neil.

"Yes, the only difference is that here one can reincarnate in a few hundred or thousand years which is way less than ours. For us it is few million years however the birth and death is all in relativity of time in whole of cosmos!"

"Unbelievable! This is just like failing in class and restarting in the same class again!"

"Kind of!"

"You have so many superpowers, why don't you use them then?"

"Perhaps, I cannot! Because I am connected with my little girl who is incapable of handling so much power".

"What if I go to the *SUPREME* and help you out? You think I have a bright heart? And am I eligible with whatever lower emotions or good emotions you mentioned?"

"You still have fears, sadness and anger inside you which darkens your heart. You can't enter the tunnel with that darkness".

"Oh! I feel dejected. So, can I change the darkness with my mind?"

"It's not just your mind but it's more of your heart that can change this. Someone closer to the brightest of heart was my little girl who plunged into the path unknown to save me. But, by the time she was back, she had already lost over sixty years of her life on Earth. It was quite an ordeal for me to pull her back from the loop. I choose to stay with her even though the portals from my creator opened up a few seconds later. She lost her parents and was all alone just because of me. I could not have left her alone for the great sacrifice she did", said *Viridian* in a softer tone.

"Heart?"

"Your heart is the centre to higher dimensions, it's like a channel that you need to switch on and tune into. It takes several years to do so, however I heard of a great *Doyen* who sits with the *SUPREME* and can transform our darkness in a trice".

"All this is so strange to me and yet it doesn't feel so alien! *The Great Doyen*…..who is that now?"

"Yes, *the great Doyen* who lives where the three rivers meet, they say Doyen never sleeps! The only path is through the roots of *Zendaxiah.*"

Neil's definition of darkness took a complete U-turn with what *Viridian* said. Darkness was not the time after sunset nor the evil monsters that would attack us at night who were represented as dark in his games, stories of folklore. This was an element of den of iniquity that was lodged right inside us. Dark were our own fears, our own lies! Darkness is also choice of being unhappy while one can choose to do the opposite. Our very own habits keep sweeping us away from the right path. Peradventure who we chose to be and what we took responsibility for.

He started reflecting on his life which served no purpose to anyone, not even for himself. He wondered what he was doing, who he was, was he the *gNeil* or the Neil in the tree trunk, a sad child or a happy child, a good human or bad human! The multitude self-enquiries catechized him while he looked at himself inside the big circular television.

CHAPTER - 12

THE WEIRDO FROM THIS WORLD

"Watch out!
The trees are integrated back into one. Wow! Nothing got killed or hurt! The trees are still alive as individuals in that giant eucalyptus tree", shouted *gNeil* as he noticed Neil engrossed in his own thoughts.

The *cosmogragnator* was the tree itself providing vital conditions for *Viridian's* survival. It all felt just like a dream. Neil looked at his watch. It was 8 am on the 24th December.

"Oh wow! I have gone over thirty years back in time experiencing everything. Hey wait! If your galactic days are so longer than ours, how is it that I have experienced everything in just one hour and fifteen minutes?"

"It's the *cosmogenic bubble* that bridges the gap as you elevate to our realm", remarked *Viridian.*

"In that case we don't have time for trials anymore. You have very little time left", sighed Neil.

"Can you please take me to that little girl? We can find a way out of this".

Viridian pointed his fingers towards the giant circular screen. Few earth days had gone by, communication to the creator of the sixth petal

COCA
Cola
SALE

SHOP
TOY SHOP
HANDMADE

remained unblocked yet. It was a delightful after noon with subtle cold winds, drizzles with sun playing hide and seek behind the moving clouds, a typical climate of the Ooty which was also referred to as the Queen of Hills. Beautiful landscapes, tea plantations, lakes, damns, fresh orange coloured carrots, exotic fruits, spectacular varieties of flowers, with birds warbling over them, colourful pucca houses so alluringly aligned on the hilly range, horses, fluffy cats, nice people, pine and eucalyptus trees were embodiment of this place.

Neil was in awe with the breath taking view which he had not explored since his arrival here. The aroma of leafage beheld a tranquilizing effect on him. Few hundred meters ahead of *Viridian*'s temporary residence was a big school surrounded by vast eucalyptus trees which surely was imperceptible from the ground level.

"Hey! That's my school! I can't believe I'm time traveling!" remarked Neil.

He was learning to concentrate better to magnify his ability to control the things with his mind. However, that was adequate to get *gNeil* to fly into the school campus via the back gate. It was lunch time. Children were having lunch under the trees in the garden unlike the canteen which was their socially useful productive work room with commendable aesthetics. The colour of the school building was the same as in the year 2022. There were plenty of flowers in the pots and the aroma was magnificent. He walked towards the main entrance, sneaked through the corridor noticing all the rooms-staff room, principal's room, rest rooms, classrooms in amusement. All were the same except that there were no advanced computers in their computer lab. None of the children had mobile or GPS gadgets in their hands or pockets.

As the school bell rang, children dashed into the corridor. Strange as he detected, no one actually spotted his presence. Everyone seemed to walk through him.

"Wait! What! Am I invisible?"

He flew through each of the students, teachers, classrooms, staff rooms, and the library without being spotted.

"Wowww! I am invisible there? But How?" asked Neil.

"Well, one can project outside the body to experience things faster and better."

"Like astral travel, Woooohooooo?"

"You have a remarkable knowledge of things Neil! You could use your brain's ability better. Now close your eyes and concentrate at the centre of your forehead to feel and know what the boy over there is thinking".

"Hmm.......He wishes to play outside".

"Well right! Keep trying. As you explore, you will master it too!"

"And what about my heart?"

"You need to speak to it, to know it!"

Neil was rejoicing at his new ability to read minds, yet he was marvelled by what *Viridian* did. He sacrificed his opportunity to get back to his home for an unknown girl! He wondered how *Viridian* could be affectionate and kind hearted towards someone whom he never met before! After all, caring for someone out of our comfort zone is an indication that something is starting to change in our heart.

Hovering around the school perimeter, he noticed a girl holding a puppy in her hand near the back gate. Neil never petted any animal. His entire world revolved around games-screens-more games. Curiously, he stood beside her and watched the girl cuddling and talking to her pup.

To his surprise, the pup did respond but not in words but in colours and vibration.

“Wow! These dogs are actually living beings! This one talks!”

“Of course, the... the... they do!” stammered the girl loudly.

Neil looked around and wondered who she was speaking to.

“It’s you… cur… curl head weirdoooo! You ne... ne… nev... nevvv... never seen a dog beforeeee?”

“Can you see me?”

“Ah well! You aaa... arr... are invisible”.

“Oh yes, I am!”

“Hahahaha! Yuuu... yuuuu... You are funnnny!”

“Mmmmm! Can you really see me?”

“Well, I am preten... pretending... that I... ii..ii.. iii. can see an.. an… and hearrrrr you. You want to touch the puppp?”

“Sure”.

Neil held a real pup for the first time in his life. It was so soft, moving its teeny weeny tail with love in its eyes. His heart had started to open up.

“What’s your name?”

“Ma... Ma.. Maa... Maya, yoursss?”

“Neil”.

“Neillll……?”

Maya was very loud and she stuttered in every sentence with repetition of the words a few times before pronouncing it appropriately with stress at the end of the last word. She was in a school uniform with plaited hair falling on one side of shoulder with a few strands of hair on her forehead.

“You are not attending your class Maya?”

“I..ii… lo..lov.. love to learnnn! But I no..noti… noticcc….noticedddd this pup and came to see ittt. Okkkkkkk…come let’s ff..f..ff..find its motherrr”.

Neil felt strange. He wondered why anyone would help a random pup with no gain.

“I would never do that in my games unless I get at least 1000 bonus points”, he whispered to himself as he started following Maya.

They walked and talked, hopped and plopped until the pup barked at the sight of its mother. Perfect union that spoke the language of love stunned Neil. His eyes overflowed with tears of joy witnessing this sight. After all, he had just started to learn what it feels like to be happy.

"Oh nooooo! I..iii.... got to gg...g.. go.... back to schoolllll", said Maya as they heard the distant bell ringing. She started to run and Neil ran with her too.

The teacher had already arrived and Maya was late to the class. Neil prompted her to not go in but she went ahead.

"M..mmm.... mmmma.... may I come in teacherrrrr?"

"Where were you Maya?"

"I was fff...ffinn...finding the motherrr of the lost puppyyyyy."

The children roared laughing at this statement.

"Don't give me excuses! Go and kneel down outside the class!"

Neil, unhappy with this mockery at her, wondered why she told the truth. She could have just said something else.

"You could have told the teacher that you were in the restroom and saved yourself from this punishment".

“Thh..thaa….that would be a lieee”.

“Big deal! At least you would be inside”.

“Dad and mom t..ttt… ttoolll… told me to never lieee!”

“You are not afraid of being insulted in front of your classmates?”

“No! Tel..tel…Telling a lie to feel good in front of otherrrrss mma....maaa....makes me unhappyyyyy… bbb ..bbbaa… beea.. because I am not meeee! Now, gg… gooo from here before mm..mm… my teacher catches youuuu”.

What appeared weird to Neil now occurred as something courageous.

“She is brave! She cares. She is honest and does things because they are right to do. Ahh.. *Viridian* another level of dejection. This girl feels right but how can one be like this? Least concerned about being mocked! Doesn’t that feel very uncompetitive? I would never bring such scornfulness upon myself!”

“Hmm, means you will do everything just to please others so they perceive you are the best?” enquired *Viridian*.

“Well, thinking of it now, it feels all that would be

a perception I created about myself with insufficient realisation that I am hankering something false. Something that isn't true! Being honest is courageous! As a matter of fact whenever I lied to others, I lied to myself indeed! How did I not know this *Viridian*?"

Viridian was carefully listening to Neil as he kept expressing the self-discovery of eternal truth.

CHAPTER - 13

THE PLANT WHISPERER

Few more earth days had passed by. Neil was mastering the manifold powers of his mind. He had started to learn that a life without gadgets is super exciting than he could ever imagine. His greatest learning was knowing that to be happy he did not need any external things. It all existed right inside him, hidden behind the veil of likes, dislikes, pretensions, lies, fears and assimilated sadness which was all false. At the inception subsists life unadulterated with wholesomeness which is always joyful, honest, courageous, and creative. Maya brought in a different perspective to his life. She was more real than his games. Kind, loving, always happy and her interest in plants fascinated Neil. She knew the names of every shrub, herb, roots, plants and trees around her, as if she could speak to them.

On a fine Sunday morning, Maya was tendering to young eucalyptus trees in her garden when *gNeil* arrived.

"Hello! Hello!"

"Neillll! That's qqq..qquuu…quite a surpriseeee! Waa.waaa..whattt are you ddd..ddo..doing hereeeee?"

"I came looking for you! So, what are you doing

with these plants?"

"Ahh! I am prrr..prrrruu..pruning them to make a bonsaiiiiii. You see th..thhhhaa.that big tree over thereeee? These are hhh..hhh..her babiessss. I kkoooo....collected them and pllaa..plaaaaa.. planted in the potttttt so thh..thh...they don't get killed whh..when the lawn is mowedddd. I wa wa...want to make a eu...euuucc...eucalyptusss forest bonsaiiiiiii!"

"Bonsai?"

"Yes, the mmm..mmmmii...miniature treessss! I read a bbb..bbb..book on them ann...annn.and

started collecting the strrr..strrraa…stray saplings to experimentttttt".

"Interesting!"

"Sss…ssee, this bonsai is kkkk…kk…..combined with ssseee….seven eucalyptus treessss. Th.. thhh..they are all rr..rrr..rooted togetherrrrr".

gNeil gaped into the roots of this bonsai. There were seven straight small trees with mildly thicker trunks inside a medium sized wide tray like pot, the roots were connected with each other by an element of light. There were tiny bot-like beings of bright yellowish-green hovering around the leaves and branches. He looked around at all the trees and plants. The healthier plants had more of these bot-beings while the dried ones had very few of them. They all appeared like engineers working with complete focus to keep the plants alive and healthy. A slightly bigger and brighter being flew across, monitoring and guiding the rest of them. Underneath the mud moved a line of communication via roots which connected all the plants together. Some roots were thicker, stronger, deeper that cut through the earth holding the soil together for other weaker roots to grow. The bot-beings were around every greenling. They appeared different in colours, had different sizes on the land, in the air, and on the leaves. It appeared like a different world which was a gleaming ocean of super vibrant colours.

As Maya was pruning them, the bot beings also flew down along with the fallen branches tendering to the need of these broken branches. Every leaf the trees shed were accompanied by them until they dried up and were taken over by the land bot-beings of different colours. The cycle of life from the germination of seed to sapling to growth and then to death were all interconnected. Nothing was a waste in this creation. Everything had its own unique purpose. Every flora and fauna worked from one program in its core. They didn't resist anything, they were in auto mode.

"Maya! Don't cut them! Wait!"

"Whh..whhhh…why?"

"Don't cut them! I think they can listen to you. Try talking to them".

"Bbbb..bbb..but…I dd…don'ttt ss..seee any responsssse".

"They are responding to you! I can see them. Touch them and feel what they say!"

Maya moved her hands on the eucalyptus plants.

The bot-beings crumbled aside alongside the movement of her hands and rebounded immediately to cater to plants.

“Now talk to them! Like the way you spoke to the puppy the other day”.

Neil could now see the image of the puppy in Maya’s mind. She was reliving the entire moment. He could see her thoughts. These were wrapped in a beautiful bright rosy pink colour. This rosy pink bubble slowly nudged the bot-beings fusing into the cohesive whole. Few more bubbles without a form fused into them causing a chemical reaction which emitted pinker colour towards Maya.

“What did you do the second time? There was no form, just the rosy pink bubbles”.

“I exx…..exxxpprr….. expressed my love to themm”.

“Do it again, a little more than before!”

As the love bubbles increased in quantum Maya and the bot-beings were now in the same auric field just like the seven petals of cosmos.

“Maya, how do you want this bonsai to be when it grows?”

“I wwaaa…..wantttt them to gg..ggrrr..grow together as oonnn..one trunkkkk. Though thh… thhh…they are ssss..sseee..seven different trees ..iii…iii…want them with sppp…sppp…spiral at the centre”.

This formed a bubble again and floated towards the bot-beings. They instantly started working on bringing the seven eucalyptus trees together. *gNeil* moved his right hand through the process that was taking place. He touched the roots feeling its radiance. He remarked, “This is amazing! You can whisper to them, not in words but in a light of colours. You are a plant whisperer Maya!”

His visualization was much stronger than Maya, at least one super enhancement that games had added to his skills. He tottered and teetered to pull his hand back swiftly while she wobbled and hobbled with big, surprising eyes. At one instant all the young trees grew into the bonsai that Maya thought of. In total astonishment they both sat four feet apart from the bonsai analysing what really happened now!!!

CHAPTER - 14

BOY FROM THE FUTURE

"Hhhhh...hhhh....
how did you do th..th..that Neillll?" asked Maya scratching her head.

"I didn't! It's you who did that".

"Hhh…hhh..how could that pooooss….possibly happennn? Ths…thisss.. takes sss..seeeverrr.. several yearsss?"

"You send those thought bubbles to them and it works".

"Whh..whyyyyy did you ask me naaa.nnnaa..not to cut themmm?"

"Because they were getting hurt! It appeared you could speak to them instead of cutting them."

"Hww…hwww..how do you knnnn….kn…know all thissss?"

"Ahh.. I..I..I…"

The stammering of *gNeil* was vanquished by Maya's father who arrived there listening to the unsettled voice of her daughter.

"Baby! Is everything ok?"

"Hmm. Daa..daaaa….Daddyyyy, see this is Neillll. He is my neeee...new frienddd!"

"Ahh! So, you have invisible friends now! Where

is he exactly?"

"Hhh…hhheeeee..here! nnnnnaa….nnnn… next to me daddyyyyy! You can waaa…waaa… wave at himmmm. He likes to be inn… innnnnvvv…invisible to others I guesssss."

"Hello Neil! I can't see where you are but it's good to meet you. Maya, I need to go now. Once done, be home for some snacks with your friend".

"I don't think he can really see me", remarked Neil in a soft tone. Maya looked steadily into Neil's eyes, puzzled at his atypical comment.

"Errrr…whhh…whhhh…Why cannot he ss… ssss…see youuuuu?"

"I am not meant to be visible to anyone. It's just anomalous of you to be able to see me! I walked around your school for a long time. No one ever noticed me barring you".

Maya moved her hand to hold his wrist but it passed through him. A bolt out of the blue hit her hard at this revelation.

"Whhhh…whhhhh….What are you?" asked Maya as she walked through him.

"I am just like you but from the future."

"Fffff……fffff…Futureeee?"

"Arrrrhhhhhhh…I am from 2022".

"2022!" Maya stood still in awe.

"Yes! I am thirty five years ahead of you. But, I am here in the same city a few meters away. I study in the same school as you. You just need to relax. Alright? You and I are of the same age, just at different times. Maya look at me! Talk to me! I am sorry if I scared you".

"I … i…i…am not scaredddd! It's j..juuuu… jusss….just that I am fff….. finding it hard to accepttttt. Kk..mm…come here with meee!"

She took him inside her home.

"Thhh…thhhhhaaaa….that is my mmmaaa… maaaa….mother over thereee. Now, go nn… nn…near her, wwa..waaa…wave your hand aa.. annn..and run arounddd".

Neil did as asked. There was absolutely no reaction from his mom as if he never existed. Maya took him to her neighbour's house, crossed the roads, took him to a nearby shop but no one really noticed or heard him. She now believed he was indeed visible only to her. But what startled Neil was her analytical bent of mind, she was not scared but she was analysing by testing it. He was awestruck by her intelligence yet again.

"Ppppeeee…ppppp…peoppp….People in future don't hhhaaa…haaav…have bodies like usssss?"

"Well, we do. It's just that I'm in my astral form. I am sitting inside the tree trunk out there".

"For hhhh…hhh….how long hhh…hhaaa… have you been hereeee?"

"For over an hour".

"Hhhh…hhho…how is that possibleeeee? I hhhh…hhhh…..have known you fff…fff..from so many dayssss!"

"That's because I am operating from a higher galactic dimension where time does not exist as relative and absolute for us. It's going to take time to assimilate this. Will you come to my present home? I am unsure if you could swap the time to see it. Still, I can take you along with me. It's right here, just a few meters away."

Maya was assessing all that was happening. She was curious to learn many more mysteries about this boy coming from the future. She nodded her head and started walking with Neil towards his present home.

CHAPTER - 15

GLIMPSE OF FUTURE IN THE PAST

"Why couldn't she feel my hand there *Viridian*?"

"Well, it's for you to choose! I told you how you can control *gNeil*".

"Can I manifest anything with my mind? Can I change her stuttering?"

"Absolutely! Go and give it a try."

"Hey! One more thing. That bonsai is similar to this tree trunk and the seven spirals with nesting space at the centre, just the way Maya had in her mind."

"Hmmm."

"I feel her right in my heart. Like I know her forever just like the *SUPREME*!"

"That's because she is my little girl and you know her from the past".

"Is this your little girl? Why did you not tell me before?"

"I didn't want you to alter any course to the unknown in her past. She already has suffered a lot."

"No wonder off all the people only she could see me. What would change when it's all done? It's past? It's over?"

"Past and present are mere reflections of your limited mind. From where I see it's all continuous. Your future can be altered in the past and the present but it has definite consequences until you learn the aspect of truth. You have a choice to change everything by focus and right concentration on the particular aspect."

"If I infer correctly from my dimensionality, there is a future in the past that we don't realise often. So, if I alter the course now, I am not sure of the repercussions that will happen in future to me and Maya. So, it means that you are free from these limitations unlike us?"

"Precisely right! Your intellectual level is elevating higher than normal pace Neil, I'm impressed."

"Wait! Did you say I know her from the past? But I just met her?"

"gLook! gNeil gAnd gMaya gAre gHere, gNear gThe gEucalyptus gTrees."

Neil made an effort to reduce her stuttering, he visualised her speaking normally in each sentence and now waited for Maya to speak.

"Take a glance at those eucalyptus treessss! Even though they are individual trees, the impression

is that of one giant treeee. Do you see thattttt?" remarked Maya.

gNeil nodded his head, "Go on!!".

"I think it's some organism clustering itself into them. Is this where you are in the futureeee? Inside this tree trunkkkk?" asked Maya.

gNeil nodded again, "Right inside here is Neil."

"Oh wow! Look! It's like an alien spaceshipppp. Colourful buttons, it's circular and it does not look like a tree trunk you mentioneddd?"

Maya continued describing the alien space ship without any stuttering but yes the funny stretch at the end didn't seem to get rectified. Strange as it could be she only saw the *cosmogragnator* and nothing else. She put her finger on the orange button which opened the door to a bright bluish-purple light which was now eventuating into a human body. It was an outlandish sight and moderately petrifying.

She moved her hand towards the body as it was now turning into a jelly-like substance.

"What is this thing Neil? Is it aliveeeee?"

He turned towards her without any expression and blinked his eyes couple of times. He bent down to look straight in her eyes.

"ur gon gisg gisg ur graphg graphg hun donh gisg na ur gon drux ged".

"Errrr.....What is it saying Neilllll?"

"Hmmm......Little earthling I suppose."

"Can you speak this language?"

"Not until now".

"Van na un…".

"Hey! I don't understand your worddds! I have had an unusual day discovering crazily unbelievable things. Can I request you to communicate with me in a manner that I can comprehend it toooooo?" requested Maya gathering all the courage.

The bluish-purple being now reflected a tint of golden-greenish colour by touching Maya's forehead with his long fingers, gazing in her eyes for a few earth seconds as if he was assimilating all the information.

"I won't harm you. Don't be scared Maya!"

"I just met a boy from the future, have witnessed oddly peculiar events in past few weeks, but I'm not scared. Are you a mind reader too? Yooouuu..

are turning Viridescenceeeee!" said Maya in awe.

"Viridescence comes from these trees around."

"*Viridian* colour to purpllleee. Wow! I have never seen such a brighttt colour before. What is your nameee?"

"Unlike you, my name is not a word. It's the frequency".

"Frequency!"

"Yes, it's way higher than your auditory capacity".

"Ummmm.......Untill I develop the auditory capacity, I will call you *Viridian*. Where are you from?"

"I am from the sixth cosmic plane."

While Maya and *Viridian* were engaged in the korero of the saga, Neil noticed that *Viridian* could not spot his presence. He could see only her! Galloped into the web of questions, some enlightenment started retorting. Hovering around them for some time, he touched *Viridian*'s shoulder and muttered, "Do you know me?"

Viridian turned to *gNeil*. He gazed at him for a few seconds, spotted Neil and looked into his eyes. There was a quiver followed by garbled words

from far. Everything around started dilating as the words became transpicuous. It was the *Viridian* from the eucalyptus tree.

"No! No, no... Don't let my past see his future! Turn away from him Neil!"

The lag in the time between the past and the present could not terminate this message. As *Viridian* saw his future from his past, a loop was created where the past and the present started coiling and turtling in opposite directions. The time dilated into circular coils with Maya and *Viridian* in the past while Neil and *Viridian* in the present. The two coils start rotating in opposite direction to each other. The past was rotating faster while the present was quite steady.

"*Viridian*! It was Maya who saved you in the past and because of the anomaly of time between the planes everything here had aged. And she was the same nine-year-old! You stayed back to protect her until she was self-sustainable. But you got stuck as the gateway never opened. So, it means Maya still exists here. Is she older now? *Viridian*! Look at that! Maya's loop! It's a hyperbole! It's swivelling our loop faster now!" muttered and stuttered Neil as a lighting of revelation struck upon him.

Viridian cut open his gelatinous layer around him and set his watch like a gadget on his hand. He remarked, "No matter what happens, don't get out of this tree trunk until I disintegrate this time loop. I cannot afford to hurt you Neil. Stay right here!"

"What do you mean?"

"Those loops are temporal alignment. If they expand, both you and Maya will never come back alive! I need to stop that before it's too late."

"What about you?"

"I anyway have little time left for myself in this body. Better put it to good use", winked *Viridian* as he created a condensed and strong shield around earth to protect it.

Viridian jumped off the time loop of the present and reached the centre point of two loops. He moved his hands creating a light with the speed of 100,800,578 meters per second. It was faster than the time it took the light to reach from sun to earth. The light coils emanating from his hands bridged the whirling loops together. In a few seconds, a massive light tunnel came into existence bringing the gyration to a halt.

Viridian of past and present came face to face.

The *Viridian* of the past experienced everything while he was in his time coil with Maya. Starting from how they became friends to her great sacrifice and the present life, flash of events appeared before them. They both now had one common goal, to save the children from the rip of this coil. Both the *Viridian's* merged into one increasing the speed of light to bridge the distance between the two time loops. After all, time existed only because of the distance. As the speed of light slowly started diminishing, Maya and Neil cried out loud together, "*Viridian*……
Nooooooooooo!"

CHAPTER - 16

THE ROOTS OF ZENDAXIAH

Neil was still inside the tree trunk. He wanted to save both *Viridian* and Maya! From the flash loops of time coil he learnt that Maya could tread on the path unknown by pressing the big golden ball at the centre of the remote. Very swiftly he pulled it out with the help of the *greenlings* who made an instant ladder for him to reach out to the remote next to the screen. Thanking the *greenlings* he dived inside the light tunnel.

Looking at this Maya also jumped into the tunnel of light from the other side to pull back *Viridian* before it fell out. Neil cried his heart out not for any phone or video games but to want his friend back. Maya and Neil kneeled down next to *Viridian* who was lying down with smaller lights emanating from him inside the time coil. They sobbed in the throbbing tunnel of light.

"Go back home! Nothing will change from time for you both. I will protect you enroute. Maya and you will meet in the present", said *Viridian* in pain.

"No! I am not leaving without you *Viridiannnn.* You sacrificed the opportunity to go back to just take care of me", replied Maya with tears pouring down her eyes.

"I can't make it now. Go before this light falls out!"

"There is always a way. You said the *SUPREME* could change anything. Let's go there!" insisted grieving Neil.

"No one has ever made that path. Only the…"

"I know! The bright heart. I don't care! Help us *SUPREME*! I don't know who you are! I don't know how to reach you! I am not the one with a bright heart! But I want you to bring back my friend *Viridian* to life! I want him back home. Open your door! I will do anything you want me to in return, I will quit all bad thoughts, be nice to all, never lie, just anything that you want. *SUPREME*! Open the gateway!" Neil screamed out for help in a loud cry.

A golden-pinkish light engulfed the light tunnel inside out expanding that manifold. Maya and Neil held *Viridian* tight as the whole tunnel turned into a giant whirlpool. A magnificent golden-pink wave pushed them inside the whirlpool. They twisted, turtled, rolled, and screeched for many minutes before hitting a grassy root land.

Every single thing here was symmetrical with a unique structure and same wavelength. There was an enormous purple tree which was inverted.

It had seven roots of equal size going upward and downward symmetrically. At the centre of it was the hollow root which was thicker and larger than the rest. They stood up next to a comparatively giant frog-like creature on purple grass sitting by a silver pond. There existed just the frog with a purple beard under the light of a purple moon.

"It's you who called out to the *SUPREME*?" sighed the frog in a sharp tone.

"Yes! My friend needs to be healed. Please help!" requested Neil still sobbing while trying to settle in this new world.

A green-being with wide wings took *Viridian* under his feathers. He caressed him the way a mother would do to her baby. In a few moments, *Viridian* was back in the pink of his health. Maya and Neil hugged him with great joy. Their reunion was interrupted by the purple frog.

"The path to *SUPREME* has many more tests than you can imagine. We begin with cleaning all your dirty homes to prepare you for the journey!" echoed the purple tone in strict tone.

"But our home is not hereee", replied Maya.

"Naïve one! Your home is the body you live in.

Welcome to *Zendaxiah*! The milestone zero to the *SUPREME* begins from here", said the purple frog in stentorian tone.

"We are at the roots of *Zendaxiah*! This is where you are given the choice to brighten your heart. My dear you could enter only if you had the spark! The *SUPREME* heard you!" remarked *Viridian* while looking at them in surprise.

"How do we find our way back home?" probed Neil.

"Gratifying indeed. Come here I will show you the way", remarked the purple frog.

Purple frog made all of them stand under the roots of the purple tree. Seven gateways opened up to pass by. He continued, "These are the seven roots of *Zendaxiah*. You have to pass through each one and by successful exit you will enhance your brightness which will qualify you to meet the *SUPREME*. You will have a choice to enter first root but the next ones will be chosen by the guardians of the roots. Perhaps, when stuck only you can save yourselves. Guardians can be called upon only by the one in need. If you fail exiting any of it successfully in collective two roots time per root you will go back to the same tunnel of light in the same state in which you arrived here".

"These are too many terms and conditions!" remarked Neil.

"Didn't you say that you will do anything to save your friend?" snapped purple frog.

"This path was never meant to be easy! I will protect you no matter what happens. We have nothing to lose. Instead we all will learn!" supported *Viridian*.

"But we can't let you suffer again. Let's do this one", said Maya while holding Neil and *Viridian's* hand.

"What is a *root time*? What are these roots?" asked Neil.

"Too many questions young one hah! Very detailed I must say! Well, one root to learn and one to exit. None but yourselves to persist. No power works other than your own. Nevertheless, it's no fun until you know it yourself. Who knows you might not need all the roots to reach the *SUPREME!* Choose your path then", smirked the purple frog with a wink in his eyes.

He handed over an amethyst rock which had marked the seven roots of time for easy reference, a talking lamp to guide and a purple-coloured potion which they can use to escape the root if they could not exit within the two roots time.

They chose the pinkish-golden gateway and stepped in. After half a *root time*, Neil got stuck inside a greyish-red marshy swamp and he screeched in a loud voice.

"Aaahhhhhhhh! It hurts! It burns! It's piercing through me! Helppppppp!"

Viridian's power did not work here. Neil was in immense pain. No words and visualization helped him. Maya held his hand tight asking him to calm down as he was sinking every time he screeched.

"My powers won't work here. Remember what the purple frog said. One *root time* to learn, one to exit, none but yourselves to persist, no power works other than your own", said *Viridian*.

"It was a riddle", said Maya.

"These roots are sacred and meant to purify us. They are preparing us for the higher frequencies of the *SUPREME*. Neil, you have something to learn here. The guardian alone knows the purpose of this root. Calm down and call upon guidance", remarked *Viridian*.

Neil was taking deep breaths now. He called upon the guardian asking for the purpose of a root. A blurry slurry voice set forth in commotion moving in every part of the root and marshy swamp.

"This is the root of Honesty. You have lied many times!"

The commotion of voice stopped after this. Neil went into a flashback of how many endless times he lied through his teeth to grab mobiles, gadgets and skip classes owing to his addiction. He had lied to his friends, teachers, and parents; dishonest about missing classes and not doing homework. He wondered why no one ever taught him how important it was to tell the truth. Almost everyone lied but why was he stuck in the pain like this? What will it take to get him out of these web of lies? He was clouded by them. He wanted to set himself free. *SUPREME'S* path was of purity and courage and lies were of lower frequencies.

"Neil, remember visualization. Go, change the past right now!" guided *Viridian*.

He thought of Maya who was always honest and courageous even if it meant being ridiculed by people around her. He used his power of visualisation. He went into the past reliving every moment when he had lied. However, this time he chose to tell the truth. Some forgave him, some mocked, and one girl even slapped him. The best surprise was that his parents hugged him for being honest and appreciated him. They even gave him the gadget to play a little longer. He realised being honest was not only the best thing to do but the only thing to do. All the clouds started disappearing from his head. The swampy marsh vanished, setting Neil free from its clutches.

He felt confident, courageous and happier than before. But unfortunately, it took him three roots of time which meant that the collective *root time* could get impacted for the remaining roots. The exit door of the root of honesty opened to another unknown root.

Unlike the last time, the guardian of the root welcomed them to the root of Goodwill, Forgiveness and Balance. The trio walked hand in hand into a dark wave which encircled all three of them. They were all blinded by the darkness.

"I can't see anything!" cried out Maya.

"Remember what the purple frog said. One *root time* to learn, one to exit, none but yourselves to persist, no power works other than your own. Time doesn't exist but in the roots this is the essence. We know the purpose of the root. Let's focus!" said Neil.

"Strange! I can't see either. I never had any hostility, unkindness or resentment", remarked *Viridian*.

"I was always all of this!" giggled Neil.

"That's some honesty coming from you now", giggled Maya too.

Without any further feeling of guilt, the trio went deep within themselves to know what they had to learn here. Neil learnt how inconsiderate he was with his parents despite all they did for him from changing their location to modifying their whole lifestyle. He was always angry, sad, and stubborn. He had several unforgiving moments for not allowing him to play games, ignorant of their good intent. How his habit of excessive usage of games lead him to addiction. Every activity in life was meant to be balanced, neither excessive nor inadequate. Reviewing all his actions, he amended all in the past leading to a light which drew out the darkness from his surroundings. He learnt to forgive and promised to live a balanced life with a lot of goodwill henceforth.

"This isn't easy! Why didn't they keep these things as subjects in school?" scoffed Neil as he looked for *Viridian* and Maya.

Maya was sitting there, reflecting her learnings of how some kind act of hers stopped the learning for others. Kindness is an important virtue but one should be mindful that it does not hamper others' learning.

Viridian was still stuck in his learning. He was guilty of being unforgiving to his creator who never came back for him. He gathered up all the courage and love to let go his grief inside. After repeated efforts he finally succeeded.

He said, "I didn't know the anger piled inside me to this extent that I could not forgive my creator. Perhaps, this is the reason why I could never connect with him in the first place, I blocked the gateway to the *SUPREME* with my guilt and anger".

The time taken by them was again two *root time's* each. Even though they were concerned, a strange joy had started creeping inside them. They joyfully tackled all the situations in the next roots of commitment and sharing. They learnt that in giving one receives the most.

CHAPTER - 17

THE GREAT DOYEN

While entering the gateway of the next root, *Viridian* fell down. Everything flickered between the tunnels of light to the roots of *Zendaxiah*. *Viridian* was exhausted, with much effort he stood up again.

"Oh no! We consumed all the *root time* assigned to us!" remarked Maya in horror after looking at the amethyst crystal.

"You can take the potions and go back home safe", plodded *Viridian*.

"There has to be another way! Remember what the purple frog said. You might not need to get through all the roots to reach the *SUPREME*. We need to think. We are missing something", insisted Maya.

"Wait! I think it's a riddle, 'one root to learn and one to exit. None but yourselves to persist. No power works other than your own. Nevertheless, it's no fun until you know it yourself'. We have to do something here! It's nothing to do with *root time* or even the amethyst crystal!" Reflected Neil

"gAt gThe gPoint gWhere gThe gThree gRivers gConnect gThere gIs gSomeone gWho gCan gTake gYou gTo gThe gSUPREME gDirectly!" exclaimed the *greenlings* in joy.

"*Greenlings*, you can still get a view of us?" asked Neil in astonishment.

"I set the *cosmogenic bubble* in the guava plant to watch over us just in case you both are stuck", confirmed *Viridian*.

"Greenlinggggs? *Cosmogenic bubbleeeee*? What's going on Neeeiiilllllll?" enquired Maya.

"Maya.....err...*Viridian*, how did Maya go to your creator before? It was not these roots? She was protected by some power! What was that?" questioned Neil.

"*The great Doyen* protected her path to my creator.....The violet button on the remote...", *Viridian* said in a fainted tone.

"Wait! I was here beforeeee. What is happening guyssss? Can someone explainnn?" requested Maya.

"Well, it was you who met *Viridian* first. You helped him contact his creator. However, by the time you came back on earth sixty years were gone and you were still nine years old. *Viridian* stayed back to take care of you which cost him his life. Look, we don't have much time. I need to know how you connected back then. What took you there?"

"Wait! This means I was in my past all the time? So, I exist even now ……I did all this time travellllll……oh my god I don't even stammer now…did you just see thatttt….how did this happennnnn…?"

Maya and Neil were intertwined in the web of questions.

"What was the element which Maya exhibited in her that he didn't? Life entails such an unexpected turn of events leaving us with a plethora of questions about our own existence. All this was like a dream! How can someone powerful like *Viridian* not have a bright heart? How did the young girl do it? Maybe, the path to *SUPREME* lies in a combination of multitudes of characteristics! We are missing something! Guess! It's love which eradicates hatred! No wonder these roots were meant to teach us our true nature and make us realise the false programming of our reality. Wait a minute! Maya had selfless love which was combined with *Viridian*'s power. But he has lost his power now. Hmm. What could be the other ingredient to reach the *SUPREME*?" pondered Neil.

"*Viridian*, your heart might still be bright, now that you know it's you who disconnected with your creator. Can you call out *The great Doyen*, you said she lived where the three rivers met in the roots of *Zendaxiah*.... I think the *greenlings* are referring to the same?" enquired Neil.

"gYou gAre gAn gIngredient gToo", shouted the *greenlings*.

"The ingredientttttt.... is right hereeee!" remarked Maya.

"gAt gThe gCentre gOf gThe gSeven gRoots gIs gThe gSecret gButton gTo gThe gMerging gRivers gThat gCan gOpen gOnly gWith gThe gGleam gOf gHer gEye".

"Do something *Viridian*! Call upon *the great Doyen*!" cried out Neil as he saw *Viridian* lying on the root floor again.

"gJust gLike gYour gGames! gRemember gVisulazation. gYou gCan gDo gIt!"

"Just like the *SUPREME*, *the Great Doyen* knows and feels everything. Connect with her consciousness. Break your chain of limited thoughts! Feel and manifest it from your core which is connected to them! It's all connected", said *Viridian* in a soft tone.

A thunderbolt of realisation came upon Neil. If everything is connected, if *SUPREME* and *the Great Doyen* knows everything then all he needs to do is stop being the 'I' of everything. He was his own limitation but Maya believed in the creator's ability, she learnt who she was and hence she made it to his creator. *Viridian* limited himself by assuming that his creator's light could not be felt on another planet of another cosmic plane. If everything was connected then they were the only blockers to themselves. *Viridian* smiled as he read Neils mind. He held Neil and Maya's hand and in a blaring and roaring voice, he started humming in a strange language, it sounded like a word at first but then it was just sound and more sound and then reverberation went so high that nothing could be heard any more.

Viridian looked up with his eyes, he was only vibrating no more words could be heard. The quavering now was felt by Neil and Maya who were watching him in complete amusement Maya and Neil could feel him now, he was calling *the Great Doyen*. They could feel how connected they all were with each other. They were now speaking the language of the Doyen and the *SUPREME.*

A thunderous lightning rumbled and grumbled in the cosmic space breaking and opening the flickering tunnel and the roots to a ravishing luminescence ever known to any kind in all of the cosmic planes. It was *the great Doyen* herself who arrived to meet the trio, from the luminescence *the great Doyen* was now transforming into an embodiment of a very beautiful woman with long black hair and purplish bluish body. All the guardians of the roots of *Zendaxiah* came on the scene to bow down in honour.

The great Doyen had a perfect resemblance of love, balance and power. With a beaming smile she asked, "What can I do for your dear ones?"

"Our friend *Viridian* needs help, he needs to be home... He lost his connection with the creator and was stranded on planet earth. We need to go to the *SUPREME!* Only he can mend this, else *Viridian* will not be able to fulfil his purpose and will take many years before he begins to work on it again. We are not yet perfect to enter his abode, we lost our *root time*. We need your help", pleaded Neil as Maya nodded her head with his every expression.

"Sure!" she said in a graceful tone indicating the purple frog to make the arrangements.

"Apologies great Doyen, but they have lost all their *root time*s. I don't think they are ready to handle such a high…."

"Their great sacrifice is a sign that they can. Isn't it our job to guide them as the guardians?"

convinced *the great Doyen* in a reassuring tone.

The purple frog nodded his head and walked to the centre of the seven roots. As the purple door opened there was another pinkish golden door with the button at the centre as the *greenlings* had explained. The purple frog made his way to *the great Doyen*, she walked to the door, closed her eyes emitting a laser beam from eyes and opened the door.

"Prepare the docking stations", *the great Doyen* ordered to all the guardians of the *Zendaxiah*.

CHAPTER - 18

THAT WHO I AM

As the mystery of the docking stations started to unravel, so did the mystery of the guardians. The guardians were very powerful protectors of this upside-down tree and the roots of *Zendaxiah* which was at the very centre of the swelling cosmos and the purple frog was the record keeper of all the events in this cosmic cycle. This explained the sternness of the Purple Frog on certain occasions.

They all spoke in the language of lights and frequencies. Each guardian was specialised in certain aspects and had special super powers but the Doyen was above all. As the guardians were preparing the docking stations, the purple frog was making some notes in a paper. They were not exactly the papers but a screen like transparent gadget where all he thought got imprinted on it in a very strange script. Though very advanced and powerful in many aspects they were the most loving, kind and humble beings that Neil and Maya could ever imagine in their entire existence.

After a few *root time*, three docking stations were finally ready. They were translucent and luminous white in colour. Inside the station there was a giant tube with spray nozzles placed at equal distance at top, middle and bottom. The guardians were extracting essences from each of the roots and were adding it to the tanks that were connected to these spray nozzles.

"The atomizers… are you going to put us in those?" Neil asked with a slight unease.

"No! We just put your body suit in this until you return from the *SUPREME*", the purple frog said in his usual stern voice.

"Errr…what does he mean by body suit?" Maya probed as she delved the docking stations.

"Its kind of crazy! They say this body we have is just our home and we just live inside it" supported Neil

"We are ready for initiation, *the great Doyen*", interrupted the purple frog.

"Let's begin dear ones", *The great Doyen* guided Maya and Neil to the docking stations.

The purple frog who turned taller and broader to carry *Viridian* to his docking station was moving his head with his closed eyes. He placed *Viridian* inside the tube and verified all the three docking stations before he triggered the button on each of these. Initially there was nothing but in one *root time* Maya and Neil felt convulsions as their whole body was juddering.

They both bellowed synchronously, "aaaaaaahhhh-hhhhhhhhhh.......rarrraaaaaaaaaahhhhhhhhhhhhh-hh.....bbbbbbbhhhhhhhrrrhhhhhhhhhh".

They ran helter skelter consequential to the treatment inside the docking station.

"Stop thissssssssssssssssssss!" yelped Maya.

"Open your eyes and look around Maya and Neil", the soothing tone of great Doyen commanded them.

What they saw next perplexed them. Maya and Neil were inside the tube of the docking station which was now filled with the liquid extracts that came through the spray nozzle connected from the tanks. They looked at each other. They were pure lights outside of that tube, they didn't have a body, no hands, no legs, no face, nothing that they could touch and feel and yet could know everything that they are. They had no fears, no emotions, no thoughts, just absolute nothing and yet everything.

"This is that who you are, the beings of light encased in those bodies", interposed *Viridian* in a sprightly voice.

Viridian was a light being too, his body was inside the tube which was now gaining back its anatomy and fabric.

"Is this who I am? Light?" questioned Neil.

"Yes dear one! This is who you are from the very beginning. Light is connected to everything! In the view of the misinterpretation of fact that you mixed up your identity with *the body suits*, you started losing memory of who you are! Now you are all set to go to the *SUPREME*. Remember to take your body suits when you come back, they will be recharged after thorough clean up and you can choose how you use them when you are back on earth", replied *the great Doyen*.

Viridian was always aware of who he is but Neil and Maya just learnt their reality of who they were. The purple frog arranged a boat made of golden light for the trio to disperse to the *SUPREME*.

CHAPTER - 19

WHO DO YOU CHOOSE TO BE

As they drifted through the light, they felt a strange happiness and joy which was the depiction of the *SUPREME* itself. As they awaited their convergence with him, a show of dancing lights of various colours and length formed. Maya and Neil, who were lights themselves, touched and felt the lights. They giggled and danced in symphony with the lights while *Viridian* smiled at their joy. Life has been quite an adventure ever since they met each other. However, this sight was more than the fairy tales one could have ever imagined.

"Children, these are the light beings who live in the embracement of the *SUPREME*. They are the guardians of the cosmos", said *Viridian* pointing towards the direction of dancing lights.

The merry ride curtailed a giant bright light unknown to mankind to describe the colour or its description. After all, everything had to be felt here not in words but in frequencies of light. This was the point ZERO of the whole existence. From this spherical incandescence emerged everything in this creation. This was the creator of all the creators.

"My children! You made it home!" said the voice from the glowing light as it embraced them in its magnificent luminescence.

"The *SUPREME!*" announced *Viridian* as he bowed down in respect.

"My child do not bow down to me! You are here in my heart! All the joy you feel here is rightfully yours. I am happy to have you home!"

"Am I from you and that's why it feels like I have known you forever?" enquired Neil.

"Yes! Come all! It's the time to rejoice from all afflictions, suffering and pain you have been through".

The touch of *SUPREME* healed *Viridian*, amplifying his power several times than before. Neil and Maya were overwhelmed by this reception and the love they could never imagine. The *SUPREME* was the combination of love, power and intellect in perfect balance. The consciousness that could eradicate any opposites of this. All one needed was to open up to this mighty being who was always around but clueless we chose to stay away from him.

After many earthly days of stay in the realm of *SUPREME*, one fine day Neil and Maya were having conversation on the meaning of life.

"Here is the gleaming illuminance of all that we wish for. Down there on the planet, we are lost, unaware of who we are, and what our potential is. We were bound by the element of time which came into life because we distanced from this time ZERO which is the *SUPREME*. Wish everyone knew who they were and no one would be in agony", said Neil.

The *SUPREME* who was listening to this conversation interrupted them.

"Beloved ones! Now that you know your existential reality, you can choose who you want to be. Either you can stay here forever in my adobe or you can choose to wake up many from their dreams helping them with discernment of the unreal world of agony. I will always be with you!"

"What if we don't know what we choose is the right thing to do?" asked Maya.

"You will be guided when you ask for it my child!" answered the *SUPREME*.

"I choose to go back on earth and reform the education system. I wish to work with children and many adults and teach them what I learnt here, all of this love will help them recollect who they are", said Neil.

"So, be it my child!"

"I wish to be who I am now in the present world and work with the plants! The renowned funny, silly scientist and I will work to bring the kingdom of plants and mankind to work together for each other", replied Maya.

"You already are that, Maya. I will bless you with celestial wisdom to achieve results faster. And *Viridian*, who do you choose to be?"

"*SUPREME!* I choose whoever you want me to be".

"Wise one! I give you the responsibility of the eighth cosmic plane which is under creation. You will get your light from me henceforth".

Neil and Maya jumped in excitement when the *SUPREME* announced this. But, *Viridian* was very calm and non-reactive. In return he said, "Your will be done!"

The *SUPREME* embraced them with love. He gave Neil and Maya a pouch of four bright seeds each and a pouch of nine bright seeds to *Viridian* as a parting gift. He added, "These seeds are divine. They will protect you. And when the time is right, the seed will guide you to its true purpose."

The lights of joy drifted all of them through the

tunnels of light until *Viridian* departed in a different direction. Neil and Maya returned to the docking station to collect their body suits. They were greeted by the guardians with inordinate love. As they were back in their body suits, they felt very afresh and Maya instantly vanished from there. Viridan's body was still inside the tube which had started disintegrating as well.

"He doesn't need this body anymore, so we are disposing this one off", interjected the purple frog.

Everything around Neil was now distorted, he got sucked into the time coil again. As he woke up he found himself wrapped around by *greenlings* inside the giant eucalyptus tree trunk. It was 8 pm on the 24th December. *Greenlings* exclaimed in joy. He hugged everyone with a big thanks and ran to his home.

CHAPTER - 20

FINDING MAYA

He opened the door and jumped on his dad who was helping his mom in arranging dinner. Neil was elated and happiest as ever.

“Dad, mom, I am very sorry for causing you so much pain and I want to thank you for everything you have done for me. I could never be grateful enough for the sacrifice and love. I love you both a lot. I won’t use the gadgets anymore unless I need it for accessing any information”.

Natasha and Nirvan could not hold their tears on such revelation by Neil. They hugged him tight and kissed all over his face.

“Love you always by little boy. Come let’s have dinner”, said Natasha with tears rolling down her eyes.

Neil kept talking about meeting Maya the courageous girl and *Viridian* the powerful being. He spoke about vision of altering the education system to create a better world. He now wanted to write stories for children, some real big goals in life which were around world peace and transformation. This certainly surged his parents’ curiosity nevertheless they could not have been happier than this moment where they saw Neil so happy.

As he went talking ceaselessly, Natasha whispered into Nirvan's ear, "Though a little weird, Dr. Nair has her way with our Neil. Ever since he met her, he has never touched any games nor has he been depressed. She did something that we could never do in last few years".

"I'm seriously considering scheduling some time with her for myself", giggled Nirvan as Natasha patted on his shoulders.

They had the happiest dinner time in many years of their life.

Neil slept peacefully but he wanted to find Maya who would be older herself now. He wondered if she would remember him if he met her again in the present time, how would she look, what she must be doing.

Next morning, he woke up on his own much earlier than he would have. He ran to his parents' room and jumped inside the bed. In excitement he asked, "Mom! Dad! Do you know what a plant scientist is called?"

"Umm… You might check with our neighbour. She seems to be quite famous", replied Neil's mom.

"You mean Monster Nair?"

"That is mean Neil. You have to be respectful to all".

"Sorry mom, I am just so used to addressing her that way. But what about Dr. Nair?"

"You don't know?"

"Hmm….what?"

"She is one of the renowned botanists worldwide. Many accolades to her research. She has written several books. Oh! by the way she dropped by yesterday evening to give you the Christmas present", his mom indicated in the direction where the present was placed.

"Since when is she so kind?", muttered Neil to himself.

It was a eucalyptus bonsai and next to it was another gift wrapped in green paper.

"This is so fascinating! Do you see these spirals at the centre mom?" Neil chortled in excitement.

"Indeed, we were quite amazed at what she had made. She said that it is about thirty five years old, and she also mentioned that you would know about this much better than her".

It resembled the one that Neil and Maya had made together, seven intertwined eucalyptus

The
gEUCALYPTUS
TREE

trees. He unwrapped the gift which was a book titled 'The gEucalyptus Tree' with a note inside which read:

Dear Neil,

It was a delight meeting you and realising my own reality. Our adventure was the best time I ever had in my entire life. I chose to be whoever I'm on earth so that I could be with you, not in the past nor in the future but in the now right here. To watch over you just the way Viridian did for me all these years and relive my childhood days with you. To our many more adventures.

With lots of Love & Light
Dr. Maya Nair

"Dr. Nair is Maya!" Neil whispered to himself as he froze in a state of shock.

It all started becoming clear to him now. *The shadow girl* was none other than Maya who recreated her childhood roaming in her astral body when Maya slept. The house where Dr. Nair lives was actually Maya's parents' home, it was all here but at a different time. The sixty years were transformed by *Viridian's* creator to give her the present life. Though *Viridian* felt ignored by the creator, in reality it was his creator who was protecting him throughout.

Neil ran outside his back door in his pyjamas. He jumped over the fence trampling the shrubs and ran to Dr. Nair's patio and rang the bell continuously until she opened the door with her gaze through the spectacles that were at tip of her nose, "You trampled by plants againnnn!", she exclaimed.

Neil hugged her tight, "It's so good to have you here Maya".

Maya held him tight, "It's so good to have you here my frienddddd".

"You knew who you were on the earth in future life when we were with *SUPREME!* You could have asked for anything but you chose to stay with me! Why didn't you tell me there", Neil said with his eyes filled with tears of Joy.

"Some element of surprise is always fun my dear frienddddd! And how would you know that I wasn't as monstroussss as you considered me to be", giggled Maya

This was the beginning of a beautiful tale of friendship. Neil was more active, sharper and livelier than ever. The teachers in the school showered praises on his performance in school. His politeness and helpful nature was appreciated by his friends and teachers. His parents were proud of him. The blessing in disguise was his creativity that had elevated more than what was before. He could now draw the most complex things. He had started writing moral books for children to encourage them to be their true self based on his learnings from the adventure. Dr. Maya Nair turned out to be the sponsorer of his dream school, she invested in plans and with help of Natasha was setting out the right platform for Neil in the days to come. Maya and Neil spoke telepathically most of the time and especially when she was away on travel they would meet each other in their astral forms. Of course *the Shadow girl* had younger Maya's face now!

Everything in his life was now happier and better. However, he missed *Viridian* immensely and wished he could meet him again. Many weeks had gone by and it was a full moon night. Just like every night, he was looking up in the sky wishing *Viridian* to be next to him. That's when Maya spoke to him, "Hey Neil! I need you to pass on a message to *Viridian*. Can you note it down?"

"Sure!"

"Spotted the being under the sea at 14.5994°S, 28.6731° W"

"What being now? How can I send him the message?"

"The eucalyptus bonsai Neil! It's the gateway to *Viridian's* plane. I thought you might have figured it out"!

THE BEGINNING

TO NEW ADVENTURE

Glossary

The Shadow Girl :
A three dimensional figure which does not have eyes, ears, lips and nose.

Chattery Boy :
Dr. Nair's way of addressing Neil

TTD :
Thought Tracking Device

GPS :
Global Positioning System, a navigation device.

Greenlings :
The plants are referred as 'the Greenlings'.

Wuper Woaker Wadrozinator :
A weapon of the Greenlings

Di-Hydro Missiles :
Water based weapons of the greenlings

gHA gHA gHA gHA :
Greenlings way of laughing and they use '*g*' before every word they speak.

Cosmogragnator :
Viridian's spaceship

Cosmogenic Bubble :
Nanoscopic pellet sized gadget that Viridian inserted in Neil.

Viridian :
Name of the alien from cosmic plane which was given by Maya.

Zendaxiah :
A mythical place at the centre of the cosmos with roots upside.

The Great Doyen :
The great teacher who works closely with SUPREME.

The SUPREME :
The great creator of the creators who lives at the core of the cosmos.

The Body Suit :
Refers to the body Neil, Maya and all the earthling live in.

Root Time:
It refers to the time taken by Neil, Maya & *Viridian* to complete the tasks in roots of Zendaxiah.

Discussion:

1. What are the must have qualities to meet the SUPREME? How do you think you will develop those?
   Hint: Honesty, love

2. What do you think is the language of the Plants & Trees? Do you think they can feel, speak and express like humans can do?

3. How would you react if you found a Shadow girl? Will you play with her or be scared?

4. Where is the coordinate 14.5994°S, 28.6731°W on planet Earth? Spot it on the World map.

6. Why do you think Purple frog is strict? Do you think it's ok to be strict?

7. What do you think would be your score of good thoughts and bad thoughts if you had a Thought Tracking Device?
   Hint: Create a rating scale of 1 to 10 with 10 being good and 1 being bad

8. Discuss amongst you how many hours in a day you should use a screen gadget (mobile/TV/laptop etc).

9. Activity to do: Have two pet plants and take care of them. Write about your learnings and experience to me.

10. What do you think will be the next adventure of Maya & Neil? Do you want to be part of that?

11. Should the author write the story about their next adventure. Share your thoughts with the author at Authorvijayalathan@gmail.com.

The gEucalyptus Tree Song

Twist-ety turl-ety story
Spike-ety Yike-ety cory
Brave-ety bold-ety glory
Root-e-ty Groov-e-ty Mysteryyyyy
The gEucalyptus Tree
gA gA gA gA gAaaaaaaaa